PLAYING THE FIELD
First published May 2000 by
New Island Books, 2 Brookside, Dundrum Road,
Dublin 14, Ireland

1 3 5 4 2

Each work copyright © its respective author, 2000
Copyright this collection © New Island Books, 2000

ISBN 1 874597 81 2

All rights reserved. No part of this book may be reproduced or transmitted in any form or by any means electronic or mechanical, including photography, recording or any information or retrieval system, or shall not, by way of trade or otherwise, be lent, resold or otherwise circulated in any form of binding or cover other than that in which it is published, without prior permission in writing from the publisher. The moral rights of the authors have been asserted.

A CIP record for this title is available from the British Library.

New Island Books receives financial assistance from The Arts Council (An Chomhairle Ealaíon), Dublin, Ireland.

The Arts Council
An Chomhairle Ealaíon

Grateful acknowledgement is made for permission to reprint extracts from copyrighted material. Paul Durcan: 'We Believe in Hurling' from *Greetings to Our Friends in Brazil*. First published in Britain in 1999 by Harvill. © Paul Durcan, 1999. Reproduced by permission of the Harvill Press. Seamus Heaney: 'Markings' from *Seeing Things*. First published in Britain in 1991 by Faber & Faber. © Seamus Heaney, 1991. Reproduced by permission of Faber & Faber.

Cover design: Jon Berkeley
Typesetting: New Island Books
Printed by Colour Books, Dublin

PLAYING THE FIELD
Irish Writers on Sport

Edited by George O'Brien

NEW
ISLAND

CONTENTS

Introduction, *George O'Brien*, 9

Homers Away from Home, *Eamonn Wall*, 23

A Bit Like Shakespeare, *Mary O'Malley*, 37

Jolly Good Shot, Old Boy, *Conor O'Callaghan*, 50

Through the Grey Diamonds, *Colum McCann*, 62

Home(boy) Thoughts, from Abroad,
                              Anthony Glavin, 74

The End of the Road, *Jim Lusby*, 89

Winner All Right, *Anthony Cronin*, 102

The Butterfly and the Baby, *Ulick O'Connor*, 114

Royal, Ancient and Exasperating, *Vincent Banville*, 125

Is Football Better than Sex? *Joseph O'Connor*, 135

666 on the Devil's Golf Course, *Sara Berkeley*, 145

Contributors, 156

Here, then, we have the first main characteristic
of play: that it is free, is in fact freedom
— Johan Huizinga, *Homo Ludens*

INTRODUCTION
George O'Brien

Sport speaks for itself.

It roars in the terraces, whines through refs' whistles, grunts from colliding bodies. Bat-crack and ash-clash are its come-hithers; *boink*, *click* and *swish* its sweet endearments.

But what does it say?

That's what *Playing the Field* is interested in.

Because sport isn't only a syntax of gesture, balance, nerve and vim, no matter how pleasurably those elements score the music of what happens. It also speaks to us, for us, gives us a way of speaking to each other, to trade judgments and share common ground. We've all probably learned more than we realise from the lingos of sport: early lessons in reading body language, first instruction in the accurate use of technical terminology—never mind the fundamentals, at the very least, of the art of blaspheming and slandering with fluency and conviction! But sport also helps us play the sociability game. And isn't playing the game what sociability is all about? To do otherwise isn't cricket.

The problem is, though, that it's getting harder and harder for what sport says to get a hearing.

There seem to be so many extra voices demanding a say, so many different agencies thinking, for one reason and another, that they have to take sport into their custody. All for the good of the game, of course. Money, ever-clamorous, is

Introduction

one of the voices. The media. The Minister. The police. Advertising. Scandal.

Maybe not all of these are on the same side, and some of them are backs and others definitely forwards in the way they apply themselves. But between them they achieve the same result, which is to make it appear that the action on the sideline has to be given more attention than what happens on the field of play. So much so that just about the last thing you hear about sport is the pleasure of it, the rush, the self-expressiveness.

Supposing, though, that the fan, the amateur, the hurler on the ditch, had a voice. How would they talk back, what would they say?

There are as many answers to that question as there are fans, of course. But however many answers there may be, asking it would be a step towards attempting to address sport in its own terms. Directly. Intimately. Spontaneously. The reverse of the blues, maybe: a permissible, understandable, necessary, but very tactful, exaggeration of the daily grind. As arising from the grassroots of things. As energy, desire, affiliation. Free time, freely taken.

That's how the Select XI picked for *Playing the Field* address it.

And who better than a team of writers to talk about playing?

Writers love to play. You could say that it's by playing that they get taken seriously. The piece of writing that has most to offer — that's the best sport — is the one where play is most fully to the fore, where the writer is most fully and effortlessly on his or her game. When that happens, opposites meet their match and engage wholeheartedly with each other. All the lucky onlooker has to do is revel in how strategy has been wed to improvisation, technique has found a partner in surprise and effort becomes sublimated in delight. The result is an event memorable both for its spontaneity and deliberateness, for allowing tensions and then resolving them, for sucessfully negotiating the turf battles and risk of failure so familiar from the real world. And victory is all the more enjoyable for being so short-lived.

For the contributors to *Playing the Field,* talk about sport doesn't have to be the verbal equivalent of splendour in the grass and glorious Technicolor. Varied though their approaches are, they keep reminding us of how deeply implicated sport is in life and the living of it, in personal moments and local occasions. There's no need at all for it to be a cordoned-off realm of spectacle, stardom and cynicism. And while the focus in *Playing the Field* embraces a wide world of sports — from the field behind the house to Epsom Downs, and from a cricket pitch in Fingal to Manhattan's hardscrabble handball courts — a wider world, full of less transient challenges, is never far from view.

In 'Homers Away from Home', Eamonn Wall, new to New York, takes in his Domincan neighbours at their Sunday games of baseball and finds that what he's come across is a passport to America. A means of entry to the inner country. This place might be taken for the heart of the heart of the country—Nebraska, say, which is where the author now happens to live. But it isn't that exactly. This isn't geography. This is more an image than a place, has more to do with culture than with commerce, still, blurred though the lines may be. It's an alternative, a counterweight to the more familiar, overwhelmingly large and bright images that America projects. A green, unhurried place where men in tight-fitting outfits ('uniforms', as the locals call them) turn humdrum acts like handling, bending and waiting, into secular ritual. Formal, but not off-puttingly so; tense, but intermittently so. Not home, by any means, just a relaxing place to hang out. And in its homeliness a help in trying to feel at home.

Speaking of an inner country, maybe it was an image of some such place that Mary O'Malley got in touch with thanks to hurling. In the body rising to the ball, the body in the clear, the whippy stroke, the arcing ball, there are glimpses of a state of rare completeness. The man's world and the woman's place dissolve here. Age-old story and a youngster's imagination, the hero and Joe Citizen (make that Joan), meet and mingle here. 'A Bit Like Shakespeare', as the author says. And as the men went on with their proprietorial sports talk, a girl became her own person, dreaming of energy and grace and spirit-raising sport, finding in them the first flush of an aesthetic.

Not that there's any wish to put down that talk the men had. To do that would be to excise part of the memory tissue of a generation. 'This was below in New Ross. It was only an oul challenge match, now, mind. A young Bobby Rackard was playing corner back. And Ring comes up to him and says he, If you come anear me today I'll fucking lay you out, boy. Well, Bobby Rackard didn't give him a puck of the ball all day. Not one fucking puck of the ball.' The voice of my uncle the umpire springs unprompted from my own memory, speaking of rivalry, guts, youth, experience, guile, admiration, justice–immemorial attributes seen most clearly, most decisively, in 'the passionate transitory' (to borrow from Patrick Kavanagh) of the game.

Hurling is one sport that has never had any trouble speaking for itself, nor has it lacked for spokesmen. And probably baseball doesn't need that much introduction either. Many's the one who's played the Irish version of it—rounders; a game given immunity under the old GAA ban, if memory serves. With cricket, however, we're in another country. Rural stick-and-ball game it might be, but there all resemblance between it, hurling and baseball ends. For all its air of pastoral, taking tea and bowling maidens, never has a game been as politicised as cricket. Whether it's played in Lahore, Brisbane, Durban or, as Conor O'Callaghan recounts, Dundalk, it's going to attract some sort of power play. A hundred years ago, though, cricket was widely played in Ireland, an Ireland that, in its Anglophile way, oddly remains somewhat hidden from us.

But there's plenty of literary evidence, at least, to suggest how popular it was. In Joyce. In Canon Sheehan. In *Thy Tears Might Cease*, that fond reconstruction of the Catholic middle-class at the turn of the century. Beckett, of course, life and works. 'A somewhat crafty medium-pace bowler with a strong break-back', Anthony Cronin reports in his biography. (Beckett's first-class analysis, by the way, the cumulative outcome of two stints bowling for Dublin University in humiliating losses to Northants in 1926 and '7, is: 23 overs, 2 maidens, 0 wickets for 64 runs—less than three runs an over. Not too shabby at all under the circumstances.)

Even if it never was popular, if the best day it ever saw was when three oddballs played a game of it on the side of a hill in a blizzard, to each his own. Easier said than done, of course. As we continually learn, minorities never have smooth sailing. The chances that the attitude from which Conor O'Callaghan ironically draws his title is on the way out are probably less good than they should be. Still, I'd bet that the attitude will die out before the game does. Cricket isn't going anywhere. Why should it?

They order the matter of minorities differently in Manhattan. Or least they do on the handball courts where Colum McCann plays in 'Through the Grey Diamonds'. This is because, first and foremost, there's no 'they' on hand, no self-appointed Uncle Sam, no concept of games being foreign. (For token outsider, there's the New Jersey suburbanite.) The city takes care of the space and anybody who wants to play just turns up and gets on with it. Despite all the differences between the Latinos, the Blacks, the misfits, the women, there's every opportunity and intention for what, in the author's insight, is a 'miniature democracy' to evolve, a community in spirit, there when it's needed, for those to whom a form of community less fluid and more permanent than the game itself is not a top priority. Admirable in their self-regulation and self-containment, the courts are taken for granted.

Which is exactly as it should be, of course. But that's also what makes it a great surprise when first you come across it in the middle of the rushing, roaring city. Particularly since, although this is America, New York City, in so many ways the state of whatever art takes your fancy, these guys don't have a proper alley to play in! There's a marked-out court with a decent-looking surface, right enough. But all they have to play with is a front-wall, just like the gable ends we used at home when the big lads hogged the alley in Church Lane.

Look at the game, though, and it very soon becomes clear that, sidewall be damned, here are players. The ball moves with the speed of a squash ball, but they take it in stride. Money's at stake, naturally. Pride, too. And for many an Irish onlooker, present dissolves into past, and past becomes usable. The players are neither ghosts or strangers. If you've ever got out of the car for an hour in a country town in Ireland, you know exactly who these fellows are. It's the same the whole world over, the pursuit, the exertion, and the way the speed of the ball dispels time, space and difference.

Maybe it's just as well that the world isn't ball-shaped. That way, the ball can remain an image of a world we would like—not free of unpredictable bounces, to be sure, but inclined by its nature to roll along, giving pleasure and making friends. And maybe not just an image but an instrument, as the storyline of camaraderie running through Anthony Glavin's 'Home(boy) Thoughts from Abroad' suggests. Whether it's on the neighbourhood blacktop, the competitive hardwood of crowded city gyms or unpaved, anonymous corners of Central America, where there's a ball there's a buddy. Better yet, there's a collective buddy, the team. And then there's the champion, with whom everyone wants to be pals, though fine as winning it all undoubtedly is, it belongs in some other realm, with fate or some such metaphysical agency. It's playing that's the real thing. And learning how.

Not just in practicing, though that's the first right of passage, first taste of commitment. (Bill Bradley, American presidential hopeful, spent a lot of childhood gym-time in Crystal City, Kansas, dribbling a basketball blindfold around chairs. Imagine it.) Not just in listening to the coach, though coach is crucial, giant embodiment of all the authorities—more rigid than father, more exacting than teacher, more preachy than priest, more fearful than cop; an awesome hybrid of all of these, with a strong dose of sergeant-major, dentist and Rottweiler thrown in for good measure. But above and beyond the personal and the institutional, there are the

Introduction

teammates. Learning how to trust them. How to be a part of something, how to support, admire, how to sink into this little melting pot without melting entirely. Learning that the team works. First, perhaps most ineffaceable glimpse of utopia.

Anthony Glavin should not be understood to imply that the most appropriate symbol for the United States Peace Corps is a basketball. Not at all (though there are worse symbols). It does seem appropriate, though, that the basketball is the ball in question. It does have a sort of global look. Maybe it's just the size of it. Or those grooved lines on it—lines of the latitude and longitude of a city kid's dreams.

It's not only kids who can dream, needless to say: by definition, utopia is everybody's property. And it's not only kids who need to dream either, even if, as Jim Lusby recollects in 'The End of the Road', the odds are steeply stacked against the grown-up dreamer. Nevertheless, elusive as his dog-racing uncles may find utopia, the yen to live there for a little while cannot be denied. And, working men, they know the road to victory must, first and foremost, go the way of hard work. The grooming, the walking, the cooking, the manicuring that are lavished on the dogs may appear to be as repetitive, as demanding and as time-consuming as the daily shift at the bacon factory. The difference is, of course, that the dogs' needs are satisfied freely, willingly. Although the dogs are a full-time occupation in their own right, through being bred, trained, disciplined and nurtured to be as good they can possibly be, and as the recipients of so much devoted attention, they reclaim, justify and give expressive form to the energy expended on them. As no mere pay-packet ever could. On a road where there are so many dead-ends and discouragements—an all too ordinary, all too recognisable road—the dogs must be given every opportunity to act both as winners when the time comes at the track, and at every other time as embodiments of style, emblems of promise, harbingers of potential. As whatever may be required to keep alive even the mere prospect of independent spirit.

It's not surprising that there's hardly any talk of gambling in 'The End of the Road'. Not that the risks involved in dog-racing have nothing to do with money. But those risks come after the more fundamental ones of people with for the most part unimagined, unrecorded, undervalued lives taking a chance on themselves, with perhaps no more to go on than patience and a quick eye. And a dream of bringing home a winner.

Most of us are not in the world of racers, we're in the world of the crowd, and that's not that bad a place to be at all. Take a race meeting. There are few more vital portraits of the human carnival than gatherings summoned by horses. Think how just the names of Leopardstown, Punchestown and Fairyhouse, to take only three, are synonyms for not only a great day out and high excitement. They evoke a panorama of the social mix. Class, fashion, fortune, passion display themselves with rare, untroubled restlessness, with such a devil-may-care air that it's virtually subversive. Small wonder that Anthony Cronin, in 'Winner All Right', paints the festival of Derby Day with a bright palette. It's a genuine feast day. And not just for Cockneys, though their presence undoubtedly adds to the unbuttoned ambience. On Derby Day, all England is *en fête* at Epsom. Only a big race seem capable of creating such a phenomenon, and not even all of these actually manage it. And just listen to the crowd at the end of this particular Derby. That's one of the voices of sport for sure, as viscera and synapses release uncertainty, exhilaration, dismay and wonder, in antiphon to the horses' heightened striving.

Introduction

Remote from each other as the two events are, that Derby buzz echoes the one that catches up Jim Lusby in its excitement at the coursing meet. But—and this is the case with a lot of the contributions to *Playing the Field*, one of the intriguing results of seeing a team of writers in action—other connections bridge the distance between Epsom Downs and the meeting of hare and hounds. One link that struck me is the political. Fascinating a subject as the politics of horseflesh is, with its implications for the concept of 'industry' and its many cultural contributions (for instance to the cultivation of an image of Ireland abroad), there's a more basic point to be noted. Two different levels of politics seem to be revealed by dog-racing and horse-racing. On the one hand, dogs are the sport of the men of no property. On the other, horses are national treasures—or at least make a fair dent in the national treasury—on account of their stud potential. Not only that; there's a more complicated connection. This emerges in the contrasting images the two sports give of the social realities of need, power and choice, illustrating not so much party politics as the moral norms and cultural conventions on which the parties take their stands. In the way they do that, the dogs of Gracedieu are as eloquent as any Classics winner.

The subject of sport and politics leads directly to 'the butterfly' himself, Mohammad Ali, leading light of Ulick O'Connor's boxing reminiscences, 'The Butterfly and the Baby'. Ali, sport and politics. It's a mix that seems as distinctive and as undeniable as one of those combinations of punches with which the fighter brought strong men to their knees. But it isn't a mix that Ali invented, as the merest passing mention of Jesse Owens and the 1936 Olympics attests. Even in Ali's own case, it was the United States, through its courts, that brought politics to sport. What Ali did, of course, was fight back, pointing out, in effect, that he was entitled to a politics too. Officialdom might want things all its own way, but that didn't mean that it could have them. Much of this is forgotten now, as is how loud and obnoxious Ali could be (a strategy which surely should earn him some credit for being the godfather of rap). These days, Ali is one of America's very favourite national pets, and he obligingly turns up to lend his weight to a variety of good causes, nodding and smiling. But largely silent. And there's also silence as to whether or not that court-ordered lay-off, by causing him to have what amounted to two boxing careers, contributed at all to his ending up with Parkinson's disease.

'Ali, being a living legend, is a home-town fighter wherever he fights. The world is his backyard.' That's Randy Neumann, 'the Baby', speaking. It's 1976, and he describes himself as 'an inactive fighter'. It's not surprising. Mind you, by that time he had compiled a won-loss record of 31-6. And at one time he could boast of being the heavyweight champion of New Jersey! This crown he won in December 1971 by beating Chuck Wepner (a piece of trivia with which to astound your friends). Six months later he lost the return match, and despite his literary leanings, his acting aspirations, and his affectionate, if fickle, fans at the Lion's Head, never amounted to a whole lot after that. Cutting more easily than even Wepner; whose nickname was 'The Bayonne Bleeder' and who was Sylvester Stallone's inspiration for *Rocky*—that's a failing so unfortunate that you'd almost have to put your mind to developing it.

There was a time when boxing was referred to as 'the sweet science' and 'the noble art of self-defence'. In fact, there's an excellent book by A.J. Liebling entitled *The Sweet Science* which badly needs reprinting. Now, though, if you

Introduction

wanted to write a book about boxing, or at any rate about the heavyweight division, it would have to be called *Lend Me Your Ears*. Words like 'sweet' and 'noble', 'science' and 'art' don't really operate as effective fig-leaves any more. I think Vincent Banville's 'Royal, Ancient and Exasperating' is saying something similar about golf. Royal and ancient are all fine and large, but exasperating is the reality. As one whose only venture onto a golf course consisted of thinking that the ball called Titleist carried some deep message in German philosophy (*Tit-leist*) and of my losing as many of them as possible when my partner managed to point out my mistake through gales of hysterical laughter, I'm very well-disposed to this line of thinking.

If you ask me, golf is just some kind of moral tax that the middle-classes feel obliged to pay for attaining and maintaining their social status. A reverse of the Catholic indulgence. Something along those lines, anyway (I've been struggling for years to figure it out). Golf seems to be an outer limit of sport. For all its obviously rustic origins, it takes what can be done with stick and ball far beyond what might be reasonably imagined or expected, ventures away off out into some deep blue yonder of play, where neither the frail ideal of the team or the vulgarity of physical contact have the slightest bearing. Only such imponderables of creation like gale-force winds and unavoidable bodies of water impinge on golf. You may be playing with a partner, but the real competition seems to be with yourself. The result is tallied in greater or lesser increments of humiliation (called strokes—and no wonder) which the presence of a partner rubs in. As for spectators, they seem more incidental to the proceedings than in any other sport.

Clearly, however, I'm not the person to ask about anything

connected with golf. What with golf courses springing up like mushrooms here, there and everywhere and people in droves plunking down good money to use them, golf speaks for itself very ably. Everybody's doing it. Or at least going to the golf club. Or at the very least investing heavily in the expensive gear. And yet, even a cynical incompetent such as myself is willing to admit that there must be a thrill when the club connects and the ball sails off somewhere over the rainbow. Maybe in their quiet rage for simplicity and consistency golfers are the most stubborn dreamers of all players. When was it that golf started to become really popular? It seems to me that it was around the time that exploring space began. That makes sense, somehow.

The very popularity of golf, not to mention the big money that's associated with it, the economic punch that new courses seem to pack and the impact of new courses on their host communities provide a thumb-nail sketch of an issue that's highlighted in the last two contributions to *Playing the Field*. There's too much sport, too much to watch, too much to know, too much to play. 'Is Football Better than Sex?', the title of Joseph O'Connor's essay, sums it up.

Or so it would appear. Such a question can only be rhetorical, right? But in his book *Staying Up*, Rick Gekoski cites the case of a former player who played at Wembley once. The game was not a huge big deal, just some veterans' exhibition game. But the player in question scored. And ever after he made no bones about the way that made him feel. Years later, he recalls:

'In the locker room, I said that scoring that goal was even better than sex, so one of the lads goes and tells my missus. And when I get home she says to me, "So, better than sex, was it?" But it was, it was. Nothing like it.'

Introduction

It makes you think, I suppose.

Attempting to exaggerate exaggeration is one way to deal with the glut of sport. Another is to kill your television and invent a sport of your own. This is what Sara Berkeley does. The title '666 On the Devil's Golf Course' may have ominous connotations, but the venue itself, in the desert Southwest of America, turns out to be a much more relaxed place than many a links closer to home, as well as being infinitely more spectacular. And the author has no more designs on the place than to stare at it, spellbound, with not an earthly thought of belting a ball around (besides, the heat is stroke-inducing).

Mind you, if you do kill your television, you will end up like Sara Berkeley, and miss out on the fact that there is indeed such a sport as women's boxing; it's regularly televised; Laila Ali, daughter of Muhammad, is one of its leading lights. But in return, you may be get a pleasant reminder of the simple extemporising in which sport, competition, exercise, the leisure industry or whatever you want to call it began.

From some of the empty places of America to a customs shed in Port Harcourt, Nigeria, and from a field in Tipperary to a village in Puerto Rico, a lot of ground is covered in *Playing the Field*. And that's only the contributors' geographical range. Along the way, we note that sport provides an introduction to aesthetics and a sidelight on politics. It's a vivid touchstone of memory and commemoration, and a blueprint of a home from home. It's a bright thread in the fabric of recent social history, and a clue to a generation's evolving cultural awareness.

And through all its quirks and novelties and unpredictabilities, what sport says is don't forget to play.

Play's the thing in *Playing the Field*!

HOMERS AWAY FROM HOME
Eamonn Wall

I have sat in the Yankee Stadium bleachers as summer evenings have turned to nights, registered by the way the outfield grass turned a deeper green as floodlights replaced the sun. At Wrigley Field, home to the Chicago Cubs, I have watched umpires call ground rule doubles as balls were lost in the magnificent ivy growing on the outfield wall. Many nights, I have seen home runs hit at Rosenblatt Stadium, home of the Omaha Royals, the AAA affiliate of the Kansas City Royals, and of the College World Series. In Inwood Park in Uptown Manhattan, I often perched myself on a bench behind a batting cage and watched Dominican men while away their Sunday afternoons in intense innings of softball followed by family picnics, all accompanied by merengue from boomboxes propped on coolers. On weekend mornings in springtime, I have attended Little League to watch my son play ball under the endless sky of the American prairie. The game has taught me much about America. At its best, baseball provides extraordinary moments of contentment, and is the sport which best captures the American idea of the sublime.

Baseball is also the most democratic of American sports. If called from the stands, we would all be able to perform some of the professional ball player's tasks. I can see myself crouching behind home plate and, if I set up right, catching a slow curve ball pitched from the mound. Put me in the infield and I will be able to snare a slow roller and then fire it to first base in time for the out. I might also be able to catch a high fly ball in the outfield, and I might even be able to find the cut-off man in order to prevent a run from scoring. Sure, I would never be able to hit major league pitching, but that's not such a problem since the best hitters, on average, only manage a hit a third of the time they step-up into the batter's box. Such modest success would be impossible for any ordinary mortal in football, ice-hockey and basketball, the other great spectator sports in America. To enter a game of football or ice-hockey would involve serious risks to life and limb. As for taking on the pros in basketball, we would be just too short, too slow, too mesmerized by man-to-man marking, zone defense, and the full-court press, to make any kind of decent play.

The language of baseball is the language of life, the stuff of dreams, nightmares, and the in-between. For hitters, the objective is to make it home, a journey which can be accomplished slowly by means of crafty singles hit to various parts of the infield and outfield, or by stealth; by the well-placed bunt designed to cause confusion between catcher, third baseman and pitcher, in the infield; by stealing a base by anticipating the pitcher's high kick, or by being quick-witted enough to take advantage of an error made by the opposing team. As the Hall of Fame Yankee catcher Yogi Berra claimed in one of his famous malapropisms, 'Baseball is ninety percent mental, the other half is physical'. However, hitting a home run guarantees a quick trip home. We get through life as the hitter gets through his turn in the inning. Mostly, we make our progress like the singles' hitter, moving slowly but inexorably along from day to day, task to task, in faith that at some stage we will reach some point of completion. At times, like hitting a double, or even a triple, we experience days of great progress, while at other times, sheepishly perhaps, we take advantage of others' mistakes, and become base stealers. Then there are those days, mostly dreamed of though still within the realm of possibility, when it all comes together and we hit a home run. As we run down the line towards first, we look up and see the high fly ball heading for the centre-field wall, and just as we pass first, we raise our right hands and open our faces into wide smiles, like Mark McGwire of the Cardinals after clubbing one of his monster homers at Busch Stadium in St. Louis. We all have such days. Still, most are ordinary days. Our triumphs are small, and slowly, so slowly, we make our way home from work through rush-hour traffic and bad weather.

From the perspective of the team pitching, baseball appears equally resonant and lifelike. Here, the focus is on prevention—the other side must be stopped from getting into positions from which they can score. Again, wit and teamwork are important. Arguably, the most important figure is the shortstop, often the lightest and wiriest member of the team, whose greatest attributes are speed of body and mind. Of all the players on the field, he is the one who most closely resembles you and me. And there are days too when it can go all wrong, when the homer sails over the fence, a grand slam is scored by the opposing team. Like the pitcher on the mound beating a hopeless fist against a glove, we stand dejected, face vacant with a mixture of anger and resignation.

Though most of us now live in towns and cities, our deepest notions of the sublime are still tied up with the rural. In many respects, for better or worse, the American notion of the sublime is also rooted in the rural, which represents both an escape from what's called the post-industrial world and a reflection of it. This is why Americans look backward to Emerson and Thoreau for confirmation and to the wide spaces of the West for possibility. On a small scale, the gardens and yards of suburban American homes reflect deep held notions of such a sublime. Such ideas are part of the commonplaces of baseball, and on a profound level underline the game's continuing popularity. Baseball calls its spectators back to simpler times. Because there is no limit on how long a professional baseball game can go on for, since there is no clock involved, it is a timeless sport which brings to mind older times when lives were governed not by clocks and appointment schedules but by the more natural rhythms of sunup and sunset, and daylight and darkness. Americans schedule themselves to within an inch of their lives. Sometimes, one must wait weeks before a friend is available to meet for lunch or drinks, and it is not uncommon for parents to keep appointment books for their children, so it would be a good thing if Americans looked at the national game more closely, and learned from it.

Sometimes though, as you can imagine, long games become tedious and comedies of errors, begin to resemble dinner parties which have gone on too long, and from which there is no gracious escape. In Little League, such games become the stuff of farce. I have watched interminable innings with few hits and plenty of foul balls. When this happens, the young kids in the outfield become distracted from the game: they watch games in neighbouring fields, pick dandelions and grass, walk away from their positions to talk to each other, sit down for a rest since we all know that standing alone in the outfield is as hard on the legs as working alone in a shop or pub with no customers coming through the door. Once, I saw two eight-year-old outfielders, who were on the same team, get into a shoving match which necessitated time-out being called by an umpire and the intervention of a harassed coach. On such occasions as these, the inevitable always happens, or this is how we like to remember it. Miraculously, a high fly ball is hit out of the infield, and the fielder is completely out of position, and totally unaware of its arrival. The coach roars, runs are scored in the confusion as the outfielder has no idea where the ball is, and parents eye the heavens, and laugh. At the end of the inning, the outfielders jog off the field with smiles on their faces.

Unlike our experiences in the real world, we understand that the game we are watching will be concluded so that none of the left-over anxiety which keeps us awake at night will remain. Also, the field itself will remain unchanged and awaiting our return. In *Field of Dreams*, the turning on of the floodlights is a marvellous representation of such returns. Also in that movie, the baseball field is shaped out of and surrounded by a cornfield, emphasizing the rural essence of the sport, even though nowadays, of course, the dramas of the season are played out in large cities where the great stadiums are. The players emerge, triumphantly, from the corn. Furthermore, the Iowa ballfield of *Field of Dreams* is a natural extension of the farmhouse and the yard which indicates, quite powerfully, the degree to which the game is rooted in the pastoral and not in the heroic, as football and ice-hockey certainly are. Indeed, baseball itself is rooted in the rhythms of manual labour, involving as it does swinging, bending, being patient and keeping a weather-eye out. Also, many of the great stars are sons of the rural American heartland: Roger Maris was born in Fargo, Minnesota;

Mickey Mantle in Spavinaw, Oklahoma; and Willie Mays in Westfield, Alabama, to name but a few.

The pastoral nature of the game is, I suspect, what has made it so attractive to many generations of immigrants. Frequently they arrive in America from rural areas and find in baseball subtle nuances of the ways of living which have been left behind. Immigrants find heroes from their own places on the ballfields of America. At the end of the last century, players of Irish backgrounds became dominant in the game and, in no small way, helped the Irish find a measure of acceptance in America. Patsy Dougherty was the first player to hit two home runs in a World Series game with a pair for the Red Sox in 1903. Dougherty is also remembered for his violent temper: he was placed on waivers by the New York Highlanders (who became the Yankees) for getting into a fistfight with his manager. Joe McCarthy was the manager of the great Yankees sides of the 1930s: he led his teams to victories in seven World Series, a record which has never been surpassed. Roger Bresnahan, nicknamed "The Duke of Tralee", who was elected to the Hall of Fame in 1945, could play any position on the field. Bresnahan was a pioneer in the invention and use of protective equipment in baseball: he introduced shin-guards and the batting helmet, and added leather padding to the catcher's mask to make it safer.

However, the most important baseball player in history in terms of integration and effecting change in American society was Jackie Robinson: he was the first African-American to play in the Major Leagues this century, the first to win the MVP (Most Valuable Player) award, and to be elected to the Hall of Fame. Robinson was the first baseball player of any background to be featured on an American postage stamp. When Robinson entered the Major Leagues in 1947 with the

Brooklyn Dodgers, Leo Durocher, his manager, had to put down an attempt by his teammates to circulate a petition calling for Robinson's removal from the team on account of his colour. Robinson broke the colour bar in American sports and was an important catalyst for the Civil Rights Movement, in which he would later be active in the 1960s. One of the great emotional moments in American public life in this century was the retiring of Robinson's number 42 at Dodger Stadium in 1972, just a few months before his death. The number was permanently retired from Major League baseball in 1997, the fiftieth anniversary of Jackie Robinson's entering the League.

At the moment, much immigrant energy in America comes from Spanish-speaking peoples from south of the Rio Grande and from the Caribbean, and this is reflected in the large numbers of players from their homelands who have made their mark on the game. In 1998, after he battled with Mark McGwire for the home run crown, bypassed Roger Maris's almost mythical sixty-one home run marker, and led the Chicago Cubs into the playoffs, Sammy Sosa returned to his home in the Dominican Republic to a national holiday. If baseball reflects the rural world of home, then football reflects the hurly-burly competitiveness of the American city, something which can often be a source of confusion to the immigrant, and which can be escaped by walking through the turnstiles of a baseball stadium.

For spectators, intensity comes and goes. If you look around at a game, you'll notice people talking to each other as nonchalantly as if they were sitting together in the kitchen, or gathered on the front porch on a bright summer's day. Fans wander down the steps to the concession area under the stands to buy burgers, fries, and hot dogs, the staple food of baseball. Myth has it that Babe Ruth's diet, when he was in training, consisted of hot dogs and beer. Children keep a close eye on the vendors moving through the stand waving pink candy floss and snow cones, while adults keep tabs on the beer vendors, worried that the supplies will be consumed before their rows have been reached. Except in the playoffs, the game is not everything. And like the games, the season is long (six months of a regular season followed by another month of playoffs), so there is always time for a comeback. Of course, because the baseball game caters for the fanatic, the easily distracted, and everyone in between, it is the consummate family outing.

Failure is also part of the myth of baseball. The Boston Red Sox and the Chicago Cubs are two of America's best-loved ball clubs; in part, because of their long histories and their close associations with the cities they represent, but principally for the beauty of the ball parks and for their storied ill-luck over the years, proven by their failure to win the World Series in contemporary times. It is said that there is a curse on the Red Sox—'the curse of the Bambino'—as a result of their decision to sell Babe Ruth to the New York Yankees prior to the 1920 season. Ruth was sold for $100,000, which at the time was double the amount previously paid for a player.

Memories of the successes and failures of the Wexford hurling team in the 1960s frame my childhood. Similarly, my time in America has been defined by events in baseball. In 1986, when I lived in New York, the Mets were the talk of the town. They had dominated the National League, and advanced to the World Series after winning a memorable series against the Houston Astros. They entered the best-of-seven series against the Boston Red Sox as favourites, and all of New York, and most of the pundits, expected the Mets, led by such veterans as Gary Carter, Mookie Wilson, and Ray Knight, and powered by such emerging superstars as Dwight 'Doc' Gooden, Ron Darling and Darryl Strawberry, to win and be fêted with a ticker-tape parade. However, the Red Sox, led by their great pitcher Roger Clemens, were strong and in the driving seat most of the way.

We settled in to watch Game Six full of fear. The Red Sox were up three games to two, so if they won this game in New York the series was theirs and the curse of Babe Ruth would be finally put to rest. The Red Sox led throughout the game. With two outs, two strikes on Mookie Wilson in the ninth inning, I remember the camera shifting to the Red Sox bench to show the players ready to charge onto the field to celebrate victory. Mookie and the Mets were only one strike away from destruction. Then, after Wilson had fouled-off a number of pitches, he hit a slow roller towards first base which we all expected first baseman Bill Buckner to field and step on the bag for the final out. Then the unthinkable happened. The ball rolled harmlessly through Buckner's legs, Wilson was safe, the Mets came back and won Games Six and Seven, and thus the Series. Those October nights climaxed the end of a great season of baseball.

That summer I made another great discovery about baseball when I found that the perfect way to experience a game, if I couldn't get out to the ballpark, was by listening to it on WFAN, an all-sports radio station. Many evenings, as I was doing the dishes, or reading, I would turn the radio on and listen to Bob Murphy call games at Shea Stadium. I loved his sense of calm, his wisdom, and how his voice was such a spur to the imagination. And radio does make you imagine more, and can indeed make of the game even more than what occurs on the field. Also, I suppose, this experience brought me back to the world of childhood, Wexford summer Sundays with the purple and gold performing in Croke Park, all conducted by Micheal O'Heihir on Radio Eireann.

1998 was a banner year. It began with a proposition: would Mark McGwire be able to surpass Roger Maris's home run record? Would it be finally possible for a hitter to break a durable record which had stood since 1961? Of course what made the contest so memorable was that both McGwire and Sammy Sosa went earnestly after the record and both surpassed Maris's total, with McGwire ending up on top with a new record—70 home runs. At times in August and September, as they approached the mark, the chase dominated public life in America. The contest was great for the image of the game, as it brought new fans and because both McGwire and Sosa turned out to be such likeable and decent people. On summer evenings, I planned the cooking of the evening meal around the baseball schedule. If either the Cardinals or the Cubs were playing early, then we ate early. If the games were being played on the West Coast, I cooked in a leisurely manner, and had plenty of time for doing the dishes. Because baseball is played in four different time zones in America, this planning was a complex business, at least for me. If the television was occupied at home—not even McGwire and Sosa could compete with Seinfeld and Frazier re-runs in our house—I went to the bar. I watched it all. I loved it all. I drank gallons of beer. I'll never forget it.

When it was all over, in a lovely gesture, McGwire the victor argued that it was Sosa, not he, who should be voted the Most Valuable Player in baseball as Sosa had had more runs batted in and had led the Chicago Cubs into the playoffs. Although it was impossible for me honestly to favour one of

these great guys over the other, my loyalties were quietly with
Sammy Sosa. I had spent eight years in New York City living
in a Dominican neighbourhood and had grown to love these
island people, their music and their food, to such an extent
that I had begun to feel one of them. Also, I felt a loyalty to
and a pride in Sosa's accomplishments. Like myself, he is an
immigrant in a culture where immigrants have become
unpopular. In recent years, both federal and some state
governments have passed legislation aimed at making
America less accessible to immigrants, and have sought to
limit the benefits available to legal residents like myself.
Frequently, the immigrant is cast as a sponge on society's
coffers. One of Sammy Sosa's achievements has been to
remind Americans that their country is still a melting pot, and
that immigrants continue to bring great gifts, benefits, pride
and leadership to America. When the season was over, Mark
McGwire got his wish: Sammy Sosa was voted the Most
Valuable Player in the National League.

The other great highlight of the 1998 season was the
achievements of the New York Yankees, who won 125 games
in all, including the regular and post-seasons, culminating in
a four-game sweep of an excellent San Diego Padres side in
the World Series. As a result of those accomplishments, many
experienced pundits have expressed the opinion that this is
the greatest team in history. The Yankees achieved their
success without the benefit of a monster year from an
individual whose feats carried the team. To be sure, they had
superstars on their roster; however, the team was carried by
many and not by a few. It was an education to observe the
extent to which individual ability was absorbed fully into
team spirit, and I suppose the reasons for this were two-fold.
First, the Yankees had not managed to repeat as champions in

1997 so, as a team and to a man, they felt they had something to prove. Second, in Joe Torre, their genial and weathered manager, they were led by a man who quietly fostered calm leadership which settled the team and protected them from the notorious bluster of their impetuous and verbose owner, George Steinbrenner.

In moments of crisis during the season, a player would step forward for a day and rescue the team from peril. At times, it was a veteran pitcher like David Cone. The hitters hit consistently and for high average—led by centre-fielder Bernie Williams who won the American League batting title with a .339 average, which means that he got a hit a little more than a third of the time—and Mariano Rivera, who came on to pitch the final innings of games, and was virtually unhittable all season. Rivera, tall, slim, his face full of concentration on the mound, throws the baseball at more than 90 miles an hour. He was my favourite player on the team. I eagerly awaited his appearance on the mound with the game on the line and loved the power of his arm and his matter-of-fact way of going about his business. In 1998, he was the ultimate of cool, like a Western gunslinger of old.

There were some fairytale aspects to the season also, as well as elements of tragedy. Scott Brosius, the Yankee third baseman, had come over to the team from the Oakland Athletics, after a miserable 1997 season during which he struggled to hit .200, only to play brilliantly all season, ending up being voted the Most Valuable Player in the World Series. Darryl Strawberry, a giant of the great 1986 Mets team, who had gone through hard times which included trouble with the authorities, battled superbly for the Yankees till he was diagnosed with colon cancer at the end of the season and hospitalized for surgery. His illness made his teammates all the more determined, and they brought the World Series and Darryl back to New York for a ticker-tape parade, in which Darryl rode majestically in a red convertible.

When I was a kid in County Wexford, I was always reminded, when the talk came to sport, that the greatest hurling team of all time was the Wexford team which won the All-Ireland in 1955. And I was proud of this fact and I will never forget the day that Nick O'Donnell—the greatest fullback of all time—showed me his collection of medals and trophies. I was thinking of that morning that summer as McGwire and Sosa chased Roger Maris's record and the Yankees chased the World Series. This time, however, I had been a witness to the unfolding of history, and not merely an auditor after-the-fact, when the passage of time has transformed history into myth. Now, I have eye-witness accounts of baseball myth-making to pass on. As a child, I often heard a grown-up start a story with, 'I'll never forget that day in Croke Park...' Now I'll be able to tell the young folk similar stories about the great baseball season of 1998, and all the beer I consumed. Day by day, I followed the progress of McGwire and Sosa. When in the future, fans argue about the merits of the 1998 New York Yankees, I'll be able to describe exactly how magnificent they were because I was there.

There is a void in American life after the close of the baseball season. Summer, which the playoffs have stretched to late autumn, is well and truly over. In Nebraska, the leaves have begun to fall from the trees, and with the change away from summer time, the bright evenings have disappeared. The first snows have fallen on the high ground of the Rockies and are headed towards us. For fans of the game, the longer winter nights allow much time for reflection, celebration, and for lonesome thoughts of what-might-have-been. During the off-season, a lot of the business of the sport is conducted and personnel decisions are made which will be important for the following season. A footnote to the 1998 season was Rupert Murdoch's purchase of the Dodgers, engineered at the same time as his bid for Manchester United. Sport, like everything else, is certainly global, though this doesn't mean that Roy Keane will play centerfield at Dodger Stadium instead of Old Trafford. By means of astute trades and the signing of free agents, also-rans can be turned into contenders overnight, though as a result of the workings of the same process in reverse, a contending team may begin its downward spiral by its failure to hold on to, or properly evaluate, its own talent. Such activity keeps the pot boiling, and reaffirms what we all know: that spring will come and with it warmer weather and baseball. Waiting for us in the distance are players, stadiums, and umpires waiting to shout out, 'Play ball!'

A BIT LIKE SHAKESPEARE
Mary O'Malley

1

It is a winter evening, bitter and grey. The silence is broken by the cries of children at play. My makeshift hurley, the rough edges hurting my hand, shudders against the finger bones when it strikes another stick, hurting all the way up the arm. There is a hoking underfoot for the ball, a push, the stick snakes between my feet and the ball is gone. It is pucked down the pitch. Which is short and full of rocks. The other players are my sister and brother. The game is confused, there is scant respect for rules, even when they are known.

— Goal!

— Foul. You fouled. Wasn't that a foul, Daddy?

— It was not.

— You shoved me. She shoved me.

— I did not. You're a liar. And you're a coward!

The hurley brandished, a weapon. Adult intervention. I am seven years old.

Or a summer evening, towards nightfall. Children at play. A real hurley, the ash smooth and beautifully hefted, an effortless extension of the hand. Not as sore when the sticks clashed, more a ringing up the arm, the life of the tree still evident in the timber, like Ulysses's oar. The connection between the ash and the game is ancient and sacred. The

A Bit Like Shakespeare

small ball, not a real *sliotar*, is curving towards my goal. I lift the hurl, intercept the ball, pick it up on the stick, hop it and give a long puck, out of danger.

On one such an evening, in a field that has no rocks, though a small turlough fills every winter from a central spot known as 'The Big Hole', it is getting late and the air has cooled. The sky is clear and darkening so that the deep blue line that will be visible up to midnight is gaining definition over the ruined coastguard station. The Slyne Head lighthouse scans the village like radar, picks up the blip of the ball speeding towards me. I raise the hurl, nervous of missing. There is a lightening in the air, a slowing down of the ball's trajectory.

Between me and it, there is another dimension. In this endless moment I discover magic. And physics. The dimension of the present moment, which, the distinguished Czech immunologist and poet Miroslav Holub tells us in his essay of that name, lasts three seconds. I was taken aback to read this, as I have always considered the present moment, inside whose boundaries battalions of angels could be flying, or radio waves sizzling from outer space, to be infinitely elastic. More likely the latter. I was never much visited by pretty angels. 'Now I lay me down to sleep, I pray to God my soul to keep.' At that age, you expect whiteness, and gold. The ones I saw roosting at the end of my bed had the look of fourteenth-century Venetian corner boys. Distinctly fallen. I suppose they had to go where they were sent. Of course I didn't know that then. I thought I hadn't prayed hard enough. So I'd pray again: 'Matthew, Mark, Luke and John, bless the bed that I lie on', and they'd fly off into the dark that spawned them.

They'd have made lovely hurlers, with a bit of discipline.

2

Reading 'Markings', a poem about a group of boys playing football, brought the moment back to me with a shiver of recognition when Seamus Heaney's book *Seeing Things* was published in 1991.

There was a fleetness, furtherance, untiredness
In time that was extra, unforeseen and free.

Extra time. One memory of cold hands and humiliation, one epiphany. In between I must have played with dolls.

This was all at the beginning of the 1960s, before television, before affluence. Most children helped out with housework, potato picking and at the right time and on the right tide, picking winkles and carrageen. The games were hard won and not an automatic right, especially for the eldest girl, who had to help her hard-pressed mother with the child-minding. Being let out late in the evening may have added spice to a game. It certainly lent enchantment.

This was a time when much of what mattered in life was in areas that girls couldn't participate in. You learned to judge what was important according to what men talked about. This was true on the radio, in the papers and in the church. Men talked a lot about football and hurling, so I knew they were of equal status. But hurling was a game for the gods and football was thumpingly, resoundingly mortal, like the grunts of the players and the muck-heavy sound of the ball being booted down the field. One caught my imagination and the other didn't. Aesthetically, there was no contest. But it wasn't only that.

Sport stood in the same relation to my life as fishing, farming and saying Mass. These activities were fixed stars in the world I inhabited but bore a strangely tangential relationship to my life. All three were much debated, with more prominence given to one or the other according to the time of year. Thus there would be more attention given to matters canonical during Easter or the week of the Mission, while through the summer and early autumn the nightly conversation centred around the Quarter-, Semi- and All-Ireland finals. At some point around St. Patrick's Day, Galway's chances might be discussed, even hotly debated. More often than not, in the case of hurling, Kilkenny and Tipperary were the main contenders. When Kilkenny was playing, I always envisaged fifteen cats of varying make and shape, kitted out in black and amber. The centre forward might be a jaguar, the goalie a panther, the weak spot in the defence a marmalade Tom.

3

Until we got our first television, when I was about thirteen or fourteen, I had never seen a proper hurling match. The game was not played locally at adult level. We used to listen, gathered around the radio on Sunday afternoons, entranced by the dramatic skill of the virtuoso commentator, Michael O'Hehir. Slowly, he drew you in with a description of the crowd, the weather, the direction of the wind. Then there was the ritual naming of teams, a few words of praise for each county, the entry onto the field of the Artane Boys' Band. The teams would file out to cheers and applause. Then silence and the band played the National Anthem.

According to allegations currently being investigated by the guards, members of that band were subject to appalling physical and sexual abuse. I don't think any of the recent revelations of the dark underbelly of Irish life upset me as much as this, not even the story of Goldenbridge. The whole of Ireland watched and listened. Now we read that after the applause of the crowd they went back to their orphanage and were used and beaten. None of us knew, few of us asked questions, the state turned a blind eye. The culture of the time permitted us to live at an oblique angle to sadistic abuse of people who were perceived as other, and lesser, than the rest of us. This, according to several of the boys, is the terrible truth—we listened, undisturbed by any knowledge of it, to Amhrán na bhFiann. The ball was thrown in, there was a roar from the crowd, and O'Hehir's voice calmed us again for the first long puck, the pass, the gathering speed of an early attack. Almost uniquely, he had perfect pitch and measure. Meanwhile, the Artane boys walked off Croke Park into the arms of a sophisticated savage.

Since radio is creative listening, and since each had to rely on his own knowledge of the rules, it is certain when four or five of us were in the same room we were watching five different games. Some of them may have resembled rounders as much as hurling. Television changed that. The Gods had faces and very visible bodies. They didn't always move as gracefully as on radio. Many a young girl would have cause to remember Kavanagh's words—'That I had wooed not as I should a creature made of clay'—and now each of us in that room would not be playing our own variation on what was happening in Croke Park. Now, when I switch down the television sound and listen to the commentary on Radio na Gaeltachta, I think I have the best of both worlds, and I realise what a small part of the story a picture is.

But not unimportant, because it showed us for the first time the teams in motion. Young bodies at full stretch, drawing back the hurley and still running, hitting the ball full force and following through like dancers. There is no movement more beautiful or true to itself. Provided the player is skilled. Then there is tension between the shape of the rules, what may and may not happen on the parallelogram of the pitch, what curve may intersect which trajectory. It is pure delight to watch the tension between form and exuberance. Rigid formalism risks destroying the game, but talent needs honing and skill if it is to be rendered swift and true, a circus act between grace and muscle and the ability to tap a wild ball. As in art.

Then there is the physics of hurling. The game of hurling is played on a field 150 metres long and 75 metres wide, with goalposts shaped like the letter H at each end. Armed with hurleys made of ash and a *sliotar* made of cork covered with pigskin, two teams of fifteen men each vie, over seventy minutes, to get the ball between the posts, over the bar for a point and under for a goal. In between, it's all motion and poetry.

Clare, who take the game seriously, as befits a county that broke a thirty-five year curse by winning another All-Ireland before every man on the 1918 team was dead (they cheated fate by one man), had a mechanical engineer design a contraption to measure the impact of the ball against the ash, then did complicated things with maths to tell us wondrous tales of velocity, flexibility and the clash of the ash.

The conclusion of all this scientific testing was that a *sliotar* has to be very well made to withstand the number of pucks likely to be aimed at it in the average game, and that the hurley had to be equally well crafted. This application of scientific methods of quality control, as well as a cool, slick television advertising campaign indicate the almost total change of image the game has undergone in the past five years. The campaign was needed to revive interests in the game, particularly after a period when Ireland was desperate to leave behind every trace of what it regarded as an old-fashioned and, horror of horrors, nationalistic past.

4

This cultural revisionism was at its worst from the late Seventies until the mid-Nineties. Our young Europeans wanted no reminders of the muck clinging to their fathers' boots. To admit an interest in Gaelic games in certain circles was to commit social hara-kiri, almost as shocking as admitting you were a member of Fianna Fáil or the discovery of a Daniel O'Donnell CD hidden among the spreadsheets.

Beautiful motion. Perhaps much of our love of the game really is connected to a love of freedom, not in the narrow nationalistic sense of the 1940s, but its opposite, a freedom from restraint, from that straitjacket of shame and repression that has informed the body language of Irish people over the generations, through colonisation, Victorian values, a joyless Church, a rigid nationalism, and above all, the loss of the Irish language. Because hurling at its best, regardless of the spoken language of the players, is a game that throws a couple of hundred years of surface English off, and does it lightly. Its roots, its *'dúchas'*, as Breandán Ó hEither might have said, are deep in the linguistic structure that underpin what has become known as Hiberno-English. There is a synchronisation between the action of an All-Ireland final and the accent and expression of the commentator that is undeniable.

Sports writers and commentators seem to take their literary style from the wilder reaches of a Flann O'Brien satire and hurling is no exception. Where else would you encounter such hyperbole? This often has an astonishing effct

A Bit Like Shakespeare

on Irish male conversation. Men who never gave their children a word of praise were heard eloquently describing a player they had never met in terms more fitting to a Greek god than some farmer's son from Dunmore. All very well and probably even accurate—Patrick Kavanagh knew a thing or two about the epic nature of local events—but the same men would cringe in embarrassment rather than offer a soft word to their own, at least in public. And they become emotional, some even going so far as to hug one another. No such shamefulness went on when I was a child. Voices were raised and shoulders struck and I saw strong men close to blubbering on the occasion of a lost chance at goal, but decorum was observed and there was no hugging.

Is it only in the name of sport or war that our men feel safe in expressing sentiment? Can they not enjoy the brilliant, exciting *tour de force* of a Sean Bán Breathnach or Michael Ó Murcheartaigh commentary and leave it at that? Or at least hold the post-mortem in plain language. When we have endured the after-match interview, the talking heads treat us to heroes, warriors, feats of courage and sleights of hand. And attributes—speed, cunning, skill. All in great flights of overblown rhetoric. No metaphor is too outrageous when imaginations lose the run of themselves.

And they are not the only ones. Even the best commentators go over the top, often without realising it, and it is partly this that makes listening so addictive. There is always the hope of some nugget of excess. This style of rhetoric is deftly and affectionately handled by Paul Durcan in his poem, 'We Believe in Hurling'.

> *... These are the boys who were born*
> *To sweeten and delight;*
> *To bejewel and beautify.*

I laugh, I gasp, I frown.
At the final whistle I jump down to my feet,
Hug myself.

Then the action moves to the interview.

... He cries: 'The game of hurling
Is pure poetry.
Pure inspiration. Pure technique.
Hurling won the game today,
Not Tipperary, not Clare.
Today we saw the greatest game
Of hurling we will ever see.'

After the match, drink, violence, romance. The All-Ireland hurling final is always the best show in town.

Before the economic explosion of the Seventies, we lived in social conditions very similar to what Breandán Ó hEither described in Inis Mór almost thirty years before in his *Over the Bar*. There too, the only popular organisations of note, as Ó hEither calls them, were the Fianna Fáil Party and the Catholic Church, although unlike Inis Mór we also had Fine Gael supporters. There wasn't a lot of entertainment.

At ten years old the only film I had ever seen was *The Quiet Man*. Filmed near Leenane, it was widely agreed by both women and men that the best scene in the film was when nice, patient John Wayne dragged Maureen O'Hara, the strap, across a valley of a sickeningly vivid green by her flaming red hair. In glorious living Technicolor. Or so I remember it, and I certainly remember the excitement of people who had seen their own place glorified by Hollywood. I have heard this depiction of Ireland mocked, and the response of the local people gives rise to snide comments. I suppose there is always danger when we follow someone else's vision and

A Bit Like Shakespeare

expect to put on a new identity with a language, but I resent the attitude of our cultural police. Neither Conamara nor Connemara has been fortunate in the calibre of its commentators, and oh what a lot of them there are, all flogging some version of a place in whose light they often hope to reinvent themselves, and investing the place with a weight and colour it was never meant to carry. Those same commentators are only thwarted by the obstinacy of the locals, who persist in not knowing what's good for them and naming pubs after Hollywood films. I have often wondered which are worse, the blow-ins demanding a cultural purity that exists solely in their own minds, or those who have seen us as savage, noble or otherwise.

Such analysis lay in the future. I loved seeing a place I knew invested with all the style and glamour of the movies and looked down on people who came from ugly or boring places that no one would ever think of making a film in, at the same time as I dreamed my child's dream of escape. Gráinne Mhaol doing battle with the Turks, outwitting the agents of the queen, and sailing to Spain and back for wine. Then dressing up for a feast in the castle. Elysian fields, heroes, Setanta in a short tunic out of some schoolbook illustration forever on the cusp of hurtling the ball into the ravening mouth of the hound poised to attack and tear him to shreds. On the verge of the great deed that would immortalise him, but would enslave him forever as Culainn's hound.

5

I don't recall that I identified any less with Setanta than with Gráinne. Of course I would have to grow up and face the cold fact that it was hard for a girl to be hero. I knew that. It wasn't respectable. I will always be glad that my father saw no reason to appraise me of this before he had to, and then only by way of caution when I was in University. Neither did the master at National School, who never interfered with our mixed games of hurling, either because he saw no need to separate us by gender or more likely because we hadn't enough pupils to play even a half-decent game unless girls and boys were mixed.

So I killed the hound and hunted the deer and felt Ferdia's agony when the friendship sundered on the plains of Ulster. Of course I was aware that this was a man's game. But wasn't everything that was worth doing? What is certain is that when I ran down the pitch at Croke Park, hopped the ball expertly and took my chance of a long curving shot at the goal, I wasn't playing camogie. I believe I realised very early on that it was a man's world and the rules were against me. I'd ignore them and see what happened. There was nothing revolutionary or brave about this, in fact I was a very fearful child. But I was also passionate and in the war between the two, the thirst for life sometimes won out. So I think I just forgot that I was a girl or that girls couldn't play. What use is fantasy is you are bound by the rules of the ordinary?

By the nature of the game, I was excluded. I lived in a house where passion was deemed normal, even approved in my father's case. But I knew that outside of the kitchen, any remarks about a match should be preceded by a ritual disclaimer of any knowledge. 'Who'll win on Sunday?' or 'Have you a bet on Mayo?' was deemed sufficient. 'Will Galway last the first half?' would be going a bit far, apart from reeking of treason. But to make reference to a weak defence, to comment on tactics or stamina, that would be overstepping the mark entirely. For a woman. It would be greeted with polite silence, like any lapse in taste.

Ignoring the rules was as good a plan as any, but it only worked until I went to secondary school. Then I learned to play girls' games. I learned there was no escaping the fact that priests told nuns what to do, although this was partly a question of preserving the status quo and that in reality nuns ran their own shop. It would have taken a brave priest to interfere with our headmistress, who believed in the education of young women, inspired strict discipline and was kind. She believed that the daughters of fishermen and small farmers were as entitled to an education as the *petit bourgeoisie* of the West. She believed me when I said I wanted to go to University and sorted out the endless bureaucracy of application forms. Otherwise I certainly couldn't have gone, because to this day the sight of an official form sends me into mental paralysis. I have a lot to thank her for. However, the subject of camogie didn't arise, as far as I recall. I played hockey eagerly but without passion, and the few away games only served to underline the relative social superiority of the other schools, who provided oranges to suck at half-time.

I left home and went to University, into a heady ferment of drama, literature and late-night discussions. Into a world as different as the other dimension I had glimpsed in the field by the sea. I struggled between where I came from and where I wanted to go. Not that I saw any contradictions, but many did. This involved a certain amount of trying out new ideas, rejecting others. After college, I went abroad and lived very much as part of the Portugese society in which I found myself. I felt no need for expatriate Irish groupings, in fact I enjoyed being in a different culture with different reference points. This was still the post-revolutionary period, when politics was exciting and new.

One way or another, for years I never watched a game. Then, returning from ten years abroad, I tuned in gradually to the talk of whose chances were favoured in what match. I began to realise the game had all the elements of the style and complexity of a bardic poem.

I am a dilettante, unworthy of even a passing glance from a proper fan. Yet I harbour the dream that one day I will get tickets for a final in Croke Park. But only if I am taking the place of some fickle corporate follower of fashion, and not someone who has sat on the sides of country ditches, weathering like an old hawthorn bush, all for the sake of watching a few youngsters slither and slide through seventy minutes of clumsy, unbeautiful turmoil and emerge bloody and filthy at the end.

But I want to go, as much for the chance to see Irish men impassioned and liberated by physical grace, when the parallelogram of Croke Park is transformed into a Universe of near perfect symmetry, one that moves not towards the ever-possible chaos, but governed by laws of mass and motion held in almost perfect order, as for the game itself. If I'm lucky, if the old gods are guiding play and Macha is on duty, she will have conspired to bring onto the pitch those young men whose Latin souls trapped in Northern bodies lend the game a grace and speed that make it legendary.

Flann O'Brien would approve, I think. A little hyperbole never killed anyone. At any rate, a good game provides what Frost demanded of the true poem: '... not necessarily a great clarification ... but a momentary stay against confusion'.

And so we watch, season after season, year after year, and never tire of the endless permutations of two teams of fifteen men giving us yet another staging of an old play, hopeful each time that this will be an inspiring, even a unique performance.

A bit like Shakespeare.

JOLLY GOOD SHOT, OLD BOY
Conor O'Callaghan

The night after I got my Leaving Cert results in August, 1985, a gang of us went to Carlingford, got drunk on a few bottles of Satzenbrau, and slept three to a single tent in the garden of my best mate's family's summer house. Next morning I was up and out before any of the others. My mate's father had a clothes shop in Dundalk, so I asked him for a lift. I told him that my brother Ian, who had been working in an Italian restaurant in Cape Cod for the summer, was coming home that very day. He was getting in at some daft time. I wanted to be there to meet him. I was lying. I was going home to catch the first morning of the last test to decide the Ashes. He dropped me off at the square. I walked the couple of miles to our house and arrived in enough time to make some toasted batch and a mug of Nescafé and see Graham Gooch bang Craig McDermott through the covers first cherry, to the roars of a packed Oval in blistering heat.

It's just that I couldn't have told any of them that. They wouldn't have understood. It was something which I, furtively, had managed to hide from my mates and family. For a couple of summers I had been watching the test series in England and pretending not to, saying to anyone who happened to walk into our sitting room and groan, 'Ah, for fuck's sake...' that it was the only thing on and that they could switch over if they wanted to. I had spent countless nights in the depths of winter listening to broken utterances from the southern hemisphere on the old Radio 3 MW. Myself and my younger brother Neil, who was in on it too, had saved up for a Richard Hadlee ball, bought a bat in Cleary's for £11.50. I couldn't have told any of my mates. They would have called me a faggot and I wasn't and I wasn't prepared to risk any of that.

Why cricket? Why does anyone choose any sport? They just do. But if I had to give a reason I would say that cricket offered some kind of, for want of a better word, escape. Just say that certain things in our family life had gone very wrong. My three eldest brothers had left the family home. Only me and Neil, who was around eleven or twelve at the time, were there with our mother. I suppose we took to bowling windfalls at each other up the back garden as a way of forgetting those certain things. Putting it like that, it can be no great surprise that fuzzy descriptions of the gardens of Auckland, the fireworks of Calcutta, the humidity of Trinidad, the political unrest of Colombo, the mountains of Peshawar, the cool sea breeze of Perth, all seemed more attractive than what the day-to-day had to offer. Even if it meant that school reports reported that we seemed a little distracted and even lacking in sleep.

It went on like that for a couple of years. I went to college and failed after a year and dropped out. Neil left school. All the while we were living this bizarre, twilit existence which revolved around a bag soggy with the juice of cookers and bowls of thick country vegetable in the middle of the night because an umpire had called lunch on the other side of the world. Then one evening my mother came home from work and said the owner of a sports shop down the town had a cricket club and we should go to their next training session in a local park. So we did. I fell flat on my face trying to execute a text-book square cut. Neil almost caused a fatality coming in off his long run. Afterwards, the Secretary said that if we paid a membership fee of £15 each we could join Dundalk Crusaders CC. So we did.

Dundalk Crusaders CC. A bitter story which is still at the heart of several silent feuds. The club had about twelve members at any given time, and one glorious summer. We were trying to get into the Leinster League. We were going to get our own ground, pavilion, the works. In 1989 we played a season of friendlies against teams from Dublin clubs who, to be fair, were trying to encourage a new club from an area not traditionally associated with cricket. June and July of 1989 were scorchers. A handful of Louth reg. cars toured the leafy side streets of Rathmines and Terenure and Sandymount, getting hammered and plastered afterwards and believing that that was how it always would be.

We must have seemed so naïve. We certainly were on the field of play. In the lower leagues there are no neutral umpires. So, when you're not batting, you have to umpire while your team mates are. The verb 'to umpire' being a euphemism in that instance. You stand in the middle in a mucky white coat saying, 'Not out'. A Crusaders umpire, however, didn't need a second invitation to appear sporting and stick the digit in the air. Neil, my own brother, gave me lbw first ball in a match in Sandymount that summer. In the same match, our skipper went into silly mid-off for the first ball of a new batsman. We didn't realise the new batsman was their first team opener, and one of the hardest hitters of a cricket ball you could ever see. First ball up he drove savagely. Afterwards, in the dressing room, I was ticked off by our skipper because I had disappeared behind the scorebox for a pee while they waited for an icepack to be taken on for his aching groin. Some Dublin clubs even came to play us on the second pitch of our local rugby club. It was crazy, with balls flying past your ears from bowlers who were the wrong side of medium pace. I remember an old codger with Civil Service grumbling, 'Stick in a few palm trees and it could be Barbados'. We served up teas which would have fed twenty-two teams, let alone two, and still have a few scraps for a dog.

The following winter we took an hour a week in the local sports centre for indoor nets. It was around then that those of us with any shreds of talent started to become real cricketers. We had a whole day coaching session with someone who had played for Ireland. A young lad joined whose father was English and had played minor counties. It seemed every ball sent down to him came whistling back twice as fast. One of those nights eighteen people showed up, which was the most we had ever had and far too many for such a small space, though nobody was complaining. It was, however, the beginning of the end. That same night we were watched from the balcony by a couple of hard cases one of the lads said were high up in the local republican movement. And if you're high up in the republican movement in Dundalk, you're high up in general.

What could they have possibly seen that was so sinister? If they were seeing clearly, they would have seen something which couldn't have been more innocent. A bank manager, his son, a few bucks who were signing on, a window cleaner, a National School headmaster, a building society manager, someone who worked nights in the Harp brewery, a couple of students, someone who owned a battery farm and various other sundries—all horseplaying as cricketers, delighted with ourselves, slagging anyone whose stumps got splattered by a stray straight one. What they chose to see, however, was a subversive group engaging in a dangerously anti-Irish activity. Within a week a leaflet was being circulated around the nearby housing estates, complaining about the use of their sports centre for an English game like cricket.

It would be easy to exaggerate something like this. I mean, nobody was made an offer they couldn't refuse. Our permission to use the sports centre for cricket was not withdrawn. But the visit, the leaflet and a couple of phone calls which followed left no doubt our behaviour was unacceptable. It didn't seem to bother them that badminton, soccer, basketball and all those other un-Irish sports were being played there every night of the week. I mean, I didn't see anyone playing fucking handball or camogie there. They chose to draw the line at cricket, and put a bit of pressure on in a town where nobody would have any doubt where the pressure was coming from. And it worked a treat. After that, the numbers were never anything like the same. A few of the lads definitely seemed to get the jitters. Understandably, they decided not to risk, for the sake of mere cricket, a rap on the door in the wee hours.

There's something about cricket which touches a nerve in the Irish mind in a way no other sport does. Irish people have an idea of the game which is a complete anachronism. They can't get away from its imperial trappings—the school caps and flannels and pavilions and drinks intervals and teas. Most Irish people think that cricket is played by toffs in Panama hats, with names like Jeremy and Sebastian, who eat nothing but ginger cake and wafer-thin cucumber sandwiches. At least once every season, and it's usually in Malahide because the public park is right beside the ground, someone happens upon one of our matches in progress and discovers a furtive nationalism in himself which he never knew was there. He stands for about ten minutes, directly behind the bowler's arm. Just when the novelty of it all has worn off and the full meaning of what he has been watching sinks in, he picks his moment. He waits for a lull, like when the bowler is turning at the top of his run and the fielders have stopped clapping. Then, with a Scottie dog straining on a leash and his face screwed up halfway between anger and embarrassment, he shouts, 'Oh jolly good shot old boy', and wanders about his merry way. At least once every season, always the same shout, and it couldn't be further from the truth.

Irish people are deeply suspicious of anything which might undermine their absolute sense of Irishness. Cricket is top of that particular list. It blurs the lines of identity between ourselves and the old enemy. People think if you play cricket you can't be fully Irish, that there's got to be an Anglo-something-or-other a few generations back. Truth is, those lines of identity are more blurred than we like to admit. Every once in a while you come across an unlikely candidate with an allegiance which is staggering. I was in Slattery's of Rathmines in March 1990, pretending not to watch live coverage of the test from Trinidad which was only on because the barman said there was nothing on the other channels. A Dub with a bomber jacket and a fag he had rolled himself came in and said to me, 'Is Lamb out?' and I said, 'Aye', and he mumbled, 'Fuck it!' I saw the same character in the same establishment three months later, watching the World Cup semi-final between England and West Germany. Himself and his pals were perched under the telly in German jerseys, and cried for joy when Chris Waddle planted his sudden-death penalty forty rows back.

Which isn't to say you don't come across the odd type.

The south Dublin clubs have a few old stagers with extraordinary names and pre-war photographs of themselves in the tea rooms. But they are a dying breed, literally, and very much the exception. We did have one larrier who joined Crusaders during the second season. He was a proper Exhibit A if ever there was one: a young lawyer who obviously decided that cricket would be a suitable pursuit for an aspirant gentleman. A man of considerable physical presence, with a manicured beard, he arrived at his first practice session wearing a tweed sports jacket and a cravat. We all assumed he was a vet. It quickly became apparent that he had never played the game in his life, so he tagged along for a few weeks as twelfth man. One sweltering afternoon in Clontarf he was called on, still wearing the cravat, because mid-wicket had been struck with a bad dose of piles. The very next ball was blazed straight to mid-wicket and he copped it flush on the ankle. I'll never forget him lying motionless on the edge of the square and the ball lying motionless beside him and our wicketkeeper screaming, 'Get up out of that'. His ankle was broken. One of the others drove his car home for him. I saw him last year for the first time since then, at the local racecourse. It seems he had cut a niche for himself up there, listing the runners and riders over the p.a., decked out in his jodhpurs and his quilted anorak.

There isn't much else to say about Dundalk Crusaders CC. The numbers and friendlies dwindled over the next few seasons. The fact that we never got our own ground and the fact that we could never manage to win a single match, however close we came several times on both counts, gnawed. There were a few nasty AGMs in the library of the local grammar school. At the last of those meetings, the treasurer's report consisted of him throwing a fiver before the chair and saying acrimoniously, 'That's the only money I received this year'. To which yours truly suggested acrimoniously, through the chair, that members may have been unable to pay the treasurer subscriptions due to the fact that the treasurer hadn't bothered to turn up to any of the matches.

Eventually, one of the younger lads went to work in Dublin and started playing with a small club in the wilds of north County Dublin that was short on numbers. So we did too. We said it was just to get some competitive practice in while our own club was getting on its feet. Seven, maybe eight, years later and we are still there. I see some of the others around from time to time, and mostly we don't even pass the time of day. Once in a blue moon I go for a gargle with one of the old team. We start the night lamenting all those what-might-have-beens, end it with big plans which never amount to anything.

Knockbrack CC. A small field high up one of the sliproads off the new Balbriggan bypass. At the gate there's a hand-painted sign the size of a stamp. There's a pavilion with a tea room which has ivy coming through the ceiling and a home dressing room and two bogs with doors which won't close, let alone lock. On the far side of the ground sits a shed with 'Visitors' propped against its side wall. Off-season, someone's sheep have the run of the outfield. In season, with any luck, you can see both the Sugarloaf and the Mournes. It is one of half-a-dozen or so small clubs within a five-mile radius. A cricket match in these parts isn't one of those tea-parties you'll find on the pastures of Kent and Somerset. These are big mountainy men nobody would dare call faggots—farmers, barmen, blacksmiths, bookies, roofers. You get the odd ball in your ribs from a bowler with hardly a tooth in his head, and the odd twitter in your ear from fielders with butts of cigarettes stuck between their lips. In seven years there I've seen two fist-fights, one broken nose, one ball fired at an umpire, five walk-offs, and umpteen times when players from opposite camps have squared up to each other in the middle and got slagged about it in 'The Merry Cricketer' afterwards.

What do I do? I try to stay out of all that as much as I can, not out of some kind of respect for a gentlemanly game but because I know when I'm out of my depth. Apart from that, I bat. When we joined first from Dundalk, I was sure I was a leg-spinner who batted a bit. And I got a few wickets to begin with. But gradually too many balls stopped moving off the straight and too many skippers got the willies at the sight of fielders legging it towards tennis courts and adjoining gardens. Now I bat, usually at the top of the order. I can drive until the cows come home, square cut pretty well and have acquired a breezy pick-up over mid-wicket for when the push is on. I'm known as a batsman who will play his shots. I'll hit runs or get out. I won't stand there prodding and nurdling and shouldering arms. So I hit a lot of scores in the thirties and forties. I've never hit a century, but rarely miss out altogether.

Put it like this. The highest score I hit last summer was forty-five. That was in a grudge match against a club pretty close to Knockbrack with a reputation for playing it hard. It was raining, and the start was delayed by at least an hour. They batted first. By the time I opened, chasing 137, it was after six and murky and they had one young bowler who was fairly sharp. But I started well, driving him through the covers once for four and twice for three. Before I knew it I had lost count of what I was on.

There is that moment in an innings when you are around

the mid-teens and can no longer keep track of your score. It is a spell in which everything seems a blur, in which you either get out or emerge the other side of, at a point where you know that whatever happens you can't fail. It is the transition from batting consciously to batting purely on instinct. And for a time in that knock they tied me down after a fast start, putting it on a length on middle-and-leg because they had seen I was strong on the off. I was missing half of them, or just scratching the odd single off a thick inside edge down to fine leg. I had to keep saying to myself, 'Don't get out'. Then out of nowhere the quick lad pulled one down outside the off stick and, purely on instinct, I rocked back and cut him through point so sweetly I hardly felt it off the bat. Turning at the other end, I could hear someone saying, 'It's gone, it's gone', and the umpire's coat flapping four to the scorer. I was in the clear.

After that I played shots without thinking, knowing that whatever happened I couldn't fail. There were wickets tumbling at the other end. When the total crept past the hundred mark it was clear that it was going to be down to me. This was late August, about eight o'clock. Even though it was fairly grim, and even though there was going to be only a handful of runs in it at the death, and even though we were getting a right earful now and then from some of the fielders, I found myself standing out in the middle, looking at the quick lad stroll back to the top of his run, and saying to myself, 'I really love this'.

I have come to believe, however, that things can mean too much to you. Like the way you can go for so long wanting something so intensely, and then have it fall in your lap only at that exact moment when it ceases to be important. Most amateur cricketers must have had at least one moment like that, when they find themselves out in the middle realising how much they love what they are doing. The pros, by contrast, or at least the stars we see once a year when we go over to Lord's, come across as semi-literate machines with little or no knowledge or love of the game, trudging through the Long Room countless times oblivious to the beauty and history of the place. But yes, that's the double-bind of cricket and maybe all sports, the irreducible paradox. The best players, those who make the game what it is, don't make the game what it is despite having no knowledge or love of what it is, but rather make the game what it is *because* they have no knowledge or love of what it is. Or, putting it more simply, they couldn't play a ball fizzing towards their nostrils at 90 m.p.h. while basking in a dewy-eyed nostalgia for beauty and history. Professional cricketers are no different from footballers or snooker players in this respect. They seem to see the game only in terms of fitness and technique. Beyond that, they seem too absorbed in their own haircuts and footwear contracts.

Whereas I found myself standing out in the middle, saying to myself, 'I really love this'.... and then I got bowled. Too smitten with the damp sunlight slanting across the outfield, the hush which fell each time footsteps quickened onto the pitch, the trickle of distant applause for every single I skimmed down to third man. Then the bowler went wide on the crease and speared one in, yorker-length, at my toes. The ball was only two-thirds of the way down when I knew I was in trouble. Next thing it disappeared beneath my field of vision and I made a token flick towards square-leg. It seemed to happen in slow motion. I was on forty five, just five runs shy of the chance to lift my bat and doff my cap in gratitude to the fielders and assembled stragglers. It felt like an age before the inevitable clunk of leather on stump, the tinkle of landing bails. I turned immediately towards the pavilion and was all but flattened by the on-rushing keeper and slips. Behind my back I could hear the bowler shouting, 'Fuck off home ye fuckin' sap', and that particular little spell of dewy-eyed nostalgia was well and truly over.

Nowadays, there are no bowls of soup in the small hours, and only the rare game with windfalls when I take the kids up to see their grandmother on a Sunday evening. I have a family and monthly repayments among which cricket must take its proper place—on the edge. In the summer, one day of almost every weekend is given over to the chase for runs and wickets. In the winter, now, it migrates south and becomes a kind of sub-conscious backdrop to the day-to-day. I know all the scores of all the tests in progress around the world. Occasionally, I'll set the alarm an hour early to catch the last session of the day from Brisbane or wherever. The only surefire remedy I have for the glums is two bottles of stout and a few videos of Eighties tests played beneath royal blue skies. Half an hour ago, I found myself in the kitchen clipping one off my toes for four past the washing machine. After Christmas I'll start thinking about the first ball of the season all over again. You can hear, through the air, the first ball of every season. The hour will go forward. The evenings will get noticeably brighter and warmer. Some lunchtime in late April an umpire will eventually call, 'Play', and a cherry fresh from its wrapper will come humming towards me.

THROUGH THE GREY DIAMONDS
Colum McCann

Sal was down at the handball alley first thing after the snow, a shovel under his arm. Not another soul in the park on Second Avenue. Sal limped up to the wall and threw down his walking cane, began shovelling, working his way sideways, making a snowbank to the side of the court. The bank grew to about a foot high and when he was finished he sprinkled salt on the last of the ice, wiped off the green park bench, sat down and waited for us to arrive. Sal, seventy years old, cleaned up the snow like he used to clean out the bottom of a bottle of white rum.

This strange little planet of chicken-wire and wall. At lunchtime the four courts are for one-wall handball only. A third black, a third Latin, a third white. A row of older men line up at the back of the courts, watching. Maybe they see themselves when they were young.

There are two Hispanic guys in their late twenties, Angel and Lucky, with thin moustaches and ink tattoos on their fingers. They only play doubles. Their hands are calloused thick from years of the game. The ball never travels much more than a foot off the ground, even when they serve, as if there's some alternative gravity in their style. They hit winners from between their knees. When they're winning easily, they share a cigarette, tossing it back and forth between points. They can catch it without the lit tip burning their fingers. There's no mercy to their game, even when beginners come to the court.

Angel sometimes wanders off to the basketball courts to smoke dope. The smell blows back sweet on the wind. Some of the old-timers grimace with memory. When Angel comes back there's a slowness yet precision to his game. You can smell the marijuana on his skin. His eyes have a calmness to them. His friend Lucky picks up the slack. They have this Spanish slang that whips back and forth between them. They get beaten only by a black guy named Paddy, depending of course on who Paddy is playing with.

Paddy is maybe the finest individual player, covering the court in two or three leaps, winning most of his points on the serve alone. He's a mechanic; he wears one of those blue workshirts with his name stencilled on his chest. And three thick gold chains around his neck. In a TV film he'd be a crack dealer or relegated to propping up a street corner, but in reality there is a gentleness to him and he's one of the most popular ones on the court.

The old Italian Vinny is amazing. He must be seventy-five if he's a day, but he still gets out on the court and jumps around like a prayer in an air-raid. He parks his car in the same spot each day, out on the Avenue by the fire hydrant. Vinny never gets a ticket because he puts his "tin" (police badge) in the window, though he's long retired. He is the most enamoured of any young piece of female flesh that moves within a nearby radius. Even if it's match point, Vinny is first at the chicken-wire when a good-looking woman walks past. He leans against the fence, his legs and arms spread-eagled, his fingers gripped around the wire. Sometimes the women smile at the sight—Vinny, small, fat, bald and charming—as he whispers through the grey diamonds.

It must look from the outside that we are strange inmates locked between wall and wire, all of Manhattan travelling past at its insane speed, us out there, knocking a ball through the air with the ease of those with too much time. There are maybe a hundred courts in the city in total. At any one moment a thousand people are caught up in the singular geometry of a handball. When the courts at 127th Street were closed temporarily—for renovation—people came and leaned against the chicken-wire to stare in at the emptiness. And the local *bodega* was robbed seven times.

Workers from the hospital generally arrive smelling like the corridors they move through, but not Latisha. Pretty and coiffed, she has always changed out of her nursing whites. She's been coming to the courts for so long that she's simply one of the boys, but on the court her style is different—lots of loop shots and subtle flicks of the wrist. She can spin the ball so that it loses all its bounce. Once or twice she has brought her young sons to the court to hang out.

Her sons get spoiled by the old-timers who shuffle across Second Avenue to the local deli, coming back with an armful of sweets.

Latisha is sometimes partnered by the red-haired businessman who keeps his shirt and tie on while he plays. His footwork is delicate. There are jokes about Ginger Rogers and Fred Astaire. There are jokes too about Paulie, the white guy who's about a hundred pounds overweight. It's said that when he hauls ass he has to come back for a second load.

All friendly banter of course, and the jokes get recycled as the day goes on. But sometimes you have to be careful who you spar with.

Robbie is perhaps the most easily pinned as a potential psychotic. There is a dark, boyish handsomeness to him, even though he's almost fifty. But when he's angry he actually loses his pupils, so that it looks as if his eyes have had a white curtain yanked down in them. He carries each defeat around like a wound. He consistently cheats in the most outrageous way. Shots that are six inches out are suddenly on the line. When the score is 4-4 he says it is 6-4 in order to win the argument at 5-4. He calls a block after he has hit the ball astray. He shouts for a replay by claiming that the ball hit a crack in the concrete. He conveniently forgets whose serve it is. Robbie once knocked a guy's tooth out when the call didn't go his way, sneaked up and punched him first in the back of the head, then once again when the guy was down. He was ostracised from the court for months until he swallowed his arrogance and apologised. Like lots of violent men, Robbie's apologies were actually as heartfelt as his anger. Still, there's always a sense when he's around that perhaps a fight will break out. He gets right into people's faces. His muscles twitch in his cut-off tee-shirts. His eyes trampoline. Even the hard men back off when they see his pupils roll. It would be easy to laugh him off except for the fact that his curious cocktail of skill and cheating means that a lot of the time he holds the court.

It's a tough enough hour, the lunchtime hour. A lot of the players are wound up from the hassles of work, angry at their bosses, dismayed at their wages. Most of the violence is in the language. Motherfucker. Asshole. Shitheel. And, of course, the word bullshit consistently stretched out on verbal elastic, slapping against the air for hours afterwards.

You could set all the watches in the world by the way some of the old men come and go at the handball courts. Whether it's the way the door of the bagel shop swings open at eleven and Charlie steps out just as the DON'T WALK sign starts flashing; or the way Lou strolls down at six in the evening with his cigar lit because his wife doesn't like him smoking; or the way the beehive woman comes after the first drink of the day, a little red in the cheeks.

One might expect the older ones to sit on the same spot in the benches every day, but they don't. Maybe that's because they have the knowledge that sooner or later everyone becomes an empty seat. That's their law. One day an old man is there and the next day he's gone forever. So why make dying more poignant for your friends by leaving an empty seat? It's better to roam and leave your ghost in many places.

My favourite is Sal. He talks of his days of alcohol as if he were in some war that left him with blackouts every evening. Sal is a realist, he has none of that ridiculous romance that looks for things to be what they'll never be again. He walks with a limp and carries a cane. When a handball goes astray, Sal leans out from the bench and hits it with his cane. This is a peculiar skill and it seems to me that Sal must have been a great handball or paddleball player in his day—even back at the time when he was drinking two whole bottles of rum a day.

Sal claims that handball is the best way to get rid of a hangover. 'After all, the goddam Irish invented the game,' he says.

Sal and the other men sit around with their old stories and old obsessions and old dreams and even older sandwiches that they carefully unwrap when the sun tells them to. They are the lynchpin of the courts. They hold the disparate elements together. Even the young people seem to know that one of these days they'll be old too; that—when they look over their shoulders—they might be looking at themselves.

There have even been afternoons when boycotts of Robbie

were organised and nobody would play with him. This is, of course, a childish thing. But our boyhoods last a lot longer than we pretend, most of us still living out our lives in our metaphorical short pants.

'Brotherman,' says Paddy, 'you ain't seen nothing yet.' He has just hit a backhand winner from the rear of the court.

I realise now what Johnny P is shouting every time he misses a shot. It's: "Oh Rosie." It is said like a curse. I asked him who Rosie is and he said, deadpan, that it's his wife.

In the early evenings and Sunday mornings, it's racquetball instead of handball and with one or two exceptions everyone's white. It's as if the courts have changed channel. Nothing quite so odious as tennis shorts, but just a much safer feel. The tennis players are despised by everyone except themselves of course. More than once I have heard them being told to fuck off back to New Jersey. There's nothing more boring than watching a soft yellow ball bouncing flatulently on the concrete.

It's more or less the rule that the racquetball players control the two southern courts, especially if Robbie is around. Robbie intimidates with just a single stare and the tennis players leave in their expensive sneakers. The fact that nobody wants to play against Robbie, or even, with him, seems to fly over his head.

One-wall racquetball is faster than handball though the stakes never seem quite so high, perhaps because it's more housebroken, more middle-class, more reliant on equipment other than the pure machinery of the body.

In handball people have asked me to bet my wedding ring on the next match, but in racquetball everyone's much too polite to state anything but their nebulous honour. The handball player with the most finesse is an older Hungarian named Tibor. In his early sixties, his body looks like a son to his real age. Even in singles he beats the pants off twenty-year-olds. Tibor plays with the calculated indifference of an artist. He seems anarchic but each stroke is going somewhere. He is the calmest on the court and sometimes in doubles he even partners Robbie just to cool him down.

One of the other great players is Pete, who must be a hundred pounds overweight. He cannot play singles, but in doubles he kills the ball with a spectacular regularity. He is often heard to whoop. Off the court he is shy and speaks with a dreadful stutter.

Perhaps the truth of a personality is more poignantly on display in the midst of sport than anywhere else.

In handball, at least, I find this true.

Any uniform will do. Any size body is okay. It doesn't cost any money for equipment. Skin colour and class are completely irrelevant. Rather, there is an equivalence of intent. You want to win—or at least perform well. To win, your personality will stretch itself to the limits. It's fascinating to watch the cheats. When they are ahead they are incredibly magnanimous, as if they are making an act of contrition for previous sins. But when they are losing, the cheats are just outrightly brazen. I've cheated a few times, of course—everyone does—and it's an incredible rush of adrenaline to pull the wool over an opponent's eyes. It's a secret that you pretend you are whispering to yourself. Afterwards there is a horrible guilt, but by then it's too late. (I once heard Bernie say that cheating at handball was like 'cheating at sex', except you don't have to apologise to the ball afterwards.)

The rules at the courts are very simple. When you are in the middle of a game, nothing else in the world matters. Not family, not work, not politics. You play for drinks and unobtainable dreams. The only thing that matters is the next point. After a game, however, it is vital to be nonchalant, to develop the I-don't-give-a-shit swagger. You are fully on display—your anger, your jealousy, your magnanimity, your pettiness, your body, your hopes, your failures.

Sport as a weapon.

We haven't seen much of Robbie on a Sunday morning for ages. It is curious that we dislike him so much that we miss him. When a player is gone for a while, a phone call is generally made, or a visit is organised, or a rumour takes hold. We keep looking over our shoulders for Robbie. We want to see his arrogance bouncing down the street.

At first I was horrified to see the man with the hypodermic needle. He looked like he was about to shoot up. Then I realised that what he was doing was a complicated surgical procedure—filling the ball with air and stopping the gap with glue—to give the ball a greater bounce.

What to believe of this, a story told by one of Sal's friends on a lazy afternoon when the courts were quiet.

'There was a goddamn Kraut used come in here most every day, sit on the benches, not say a word to anyone. Sit there and stare away. Of course I never said a word to him. I lost a brother in Germany in '44 when he got himself a bullet in the head. They found him frozen by a fencepost. I was too young for the war but I've killed a million Krauts in my head since. This Kraut he was quiet as could be. He'd just sit down there and sometimes he'd sip on a Coca-Cola.

'And then one day—it was cold and it was only me and him in the park—we were sitting on the same bench. We looked up and in walked this old Jewish guy wearing his yarmulke. He was being pulled along by a big dog. I was laughing because the dog was really yanking this guy along. But the Kraut he wasn't laughing at all.

'The dog ran over to the Kraut and me. It started sniffing some dogshit or something at the bottom of the bench. This Jewish guy was yanking on the dog's leash but the dog wouldn't move, so he went ahead and smacked the dog real hard. I don't like to see nothing get hurt and so I was about to say something. But just then the Jewish guy's overcoat sleeve rode up above his wrist. You could see it, there, the numbers.

'And the Kraut beside me, you could hear him taking in a big breath of air down to his stomach. It was like the sky fell into his lap and he was wondering how to get rid of the goddamn thing without smashing it to pieces.

'He never came back down here, the Kraut, but it makes you think, don't it?'

Robbie has cancer of the spine. His brother-in-law came down one Saturday morning to announce it. It brought a hush over all of us, even the old men who have met death many times. Death is consistently walking off with their wives and friends. But Robbie is only fifty years old and looks so much younger.

Sal says: 'Sure he's been a pain in the ass for years, but this he did not deserve, this nobody deserves'.

The cancer is malignant and there is nothing the doctors can do about it. There is something so profoundly disturbing about hearing of an athlete who will die. As the weeks go on, Robbie stays away from the courts. It is unbearably sad. The courts were the only place that Robbie was happy and now he is denying them. He does not want to watch his old enemies jump around. The rumour is that he is in a wheelchair. The sadness and the irony—so many people have wished for Robbie's funeral. Every man he ever cheated against on the court. Every girl he's leered at from the chicken-wire fence. The guy who spat his teeth out after Robbie's big two-hearted punch. The Mexican kid he called a faggot. The faggot he called a spic. The spic he called a nigger. The guy who beat him plain and simple and then was punched from behind in the back of the head. The young kid whose bag went sailing into Second Avenue. For years, people waited for Robbie to have one pulled over on him. But never one quite like this.

Sometimes the games go right until dusk and the sun goes down behind the Empire State Building. Men and women at play from first to last. Only rains stops the games since the courts get too slippy.

There's always a group of about twelve homeless people at the rear of the court near the basketball hoops. Mostly men in their forties and fifties and one older lady who walks like a sandhill warbler. Sometimes she strolls up and down along the chicken-wire fence watching the progress of the games. There is a sense about her that once she was rich, although she never talks to anyone. At night she leaves a thermos flask on the doorstep of a brownstone house on 31st Street. In the morning it will be full with coffee for her. More and more it strikes me that Manhattan is made up of its own tiny little villages and in some sense the handball court is still the village square.

I float between a couple of courts these days—Murray Hill, Yorkville, Spanish Harlem and one indoor court on the East Side—and sometimes bring my baby daughter down to the alleys. But I find it virtually impossible just to sit and watch the games with her in my arms. I get too antsy to run out there and play. I'll leave the art of sitting down on the benches for another forty years, if I ever last that long.

Every man must grow to love at least one thing about New

York and I have grown to love these small slabs of concrete with their cracks, their graffiti, their weeds, their Parks Department insignia painted high on the wall, resembling a marijuana leaf. The walls have been here for years. Along the East River I can hear the ghosts of the longshoremen perhaps throwing down a few dollars on the next game.

The ghosts go back to other courts that I have seen—in Castlebar, in Roscommon, in Offaly, in all sorts of rural towns, even one or two in Dublin. I never played handball when I was in Ireland, but perhaps now it is my own form of ancient return, my journey back, out there during the day, with all that brutal nostalgia the emigrant gets.

Robbie died a quick death. The cancer took him in a matter of three months. In a dream I saw Sal down at the handball alley once more. This time it wasn't snow that he was clearing away, it was flowers left for Robbie by dozens of people who truly despised him. In the dream Sal was cursing the wind that blew the flowers back across the court.

Thursday morning and the court is packed. A national holiday. The sun is out over the city. The weather has kicked in early and Vinny is at the chicken-wire, licking his lips and announcing his joy at the appearance of summer nipples.

He whistles at the girl in a short skirt. She tosses her hair back in a sort of happiness, like a horse. His partner is shouting from the courts. Vinny hops back over the concrete and crouches down to receive a serve. Blue veins in the back of his legs. Liver spots on his hands. He screams at the server: 'You couldn't make shit outa applebutter, you goddamn guinea bastard.'

The serve goes past him and he loses the point. 'See,' says Vinny, 'I told ya, I told ya. Try that again.'

At the rear of the court Sal is laughing at his friend's

antics. He and the other old men are passing around the racing pages of a newspaper. A lone dog gambols in and cocks his leg against the basketball pole. The homeless woman starts singing a song about a loverman. Angel is hunched into his cigarettes. On Third Avenue there are fumes belching out from the buses and the taxis. There are sirens in the distance. They are loud and shrill. Sometimes they sound as if they are mourning in advance. Maybe that's the ghost of Robbie coming back down to annoy us.

The city is alive. The handball court is alive. Another point is about to be played. Vinny crouches down once more and mutters something about the girl in the short skirt. At the end of the chicken-wire, she looks back and gives him a smile. He grins and even manages to return the serve.

Vinny will remember this moment forever. He loses the point but, what the hell, he got the girl.

HOME(BOY) THOUGHTS, FROM ABROAD
Anthony Glavin

It was in a northside Dublin video shop this past summer that the penny dropped. Or maybe not dropped so much as bounced—like a basketball? I was staring at titles, but part of my brain must have been listening to another customer behind me, processing accent and inflection, because as that voice went out the door, something prompted me to turn and see the back of one truly tall cat, more specifically, a six-foot-seven (or so) Afro-American.

My immediate thought, of course, was does he play ball? As in b-ball, roundball, *baloncesto*, basketball. Maybe for one of the Irish semi-pro teams who import a handful of US ex-college players to lead them to Irish basketball glory, such as it is? I accept it was hardly a PC *sequitur*, but it was my first thought that evening, and I make no apologies for it. Besides, why wouldn't a tall black guy put me in mind of posting up or setting picks, given that I played on the same high-school team as legendary New York Knickerbocker centre Patrick Ewing? I kid you not, the same New York Knicks that Woody Allen makes such a fuss over, as if *he* and Patrick had worn the same maroon and white high-school uniform.

Be that as it may, the buzz from that Dublin sighting stayed with me for several days—just long enough for me to twig that I still suffer from a bad basketball jones. A 'jones', you may recall, was 1970s black slang for a heroin addiction.

What a 1950s junkie might have called 'a monkey on his back', and what has undoubtedly since been called a hundred other things. Anyhow, Cheech & Chong borrowed the idiom for their 1973 hit single, 'Basketball Jones', about this dude who had a bad basketball habit:

Yes, I am the victim of a Basketball Jones,
Ever since I was a little baby, I always be dribblin'

The song may have been a goof, but in fact there is such a thing as a basketball habit. I know, cuz I suffered one for years—an insidious dependency which suddenly last summer flashed back on me the way malaria can, making you break out in a feverish sweat even though you're miles and years from the jungle where you first contracted it.

Or in this case, thirty years and 3,000 miles away from the blacktop Russell School playground in Cambridge, Massachusetts, where basketball and I first began our ardent, albeit decidedly amateurish, affair. Though strangely, for a sport that has etched a myriad moments into memory, I don't remember my introduction to the game as clearly as I do my first encounter with baseball. That was a game between the Boston Red Sox and the Baltimore Orioles at Fenway Park, at age nine or so, where I screamed 'A home run!' every time the Sox scored. Which, for those of you who know baseball, was somewhat wide of the mark. Be that as it may, around that same age I must've realised that I'd achieved sufficient upper-body strength to heave a basketball within the general vicinity of the two net-less iron hoops attached (at exactly ten feet above sea-level) to the green plywood backboards at either end of the Russell School outdoor court. An exercise which I proceeded to repeat, spring, summer and fall, for the next eight or nine years, for even after we left the Russell for high school, we still regrouped afternoons there to play stickball, touch football—and basketball. And winters too, before the snow fell, or even once or twice after it did, spurring my best pal Danny Brennan and I to bring up snow shovels and scrape the court clean.

What I do remember right from the start, though, is trying to figure out the angles for set shots banked off those green backboards, the favourite shot of one Sam Jones (that name again!) of the Boston Celtics, who used the backboard like Alex Higgins used the cushions. I haven't seen anybody shooting off the boards from beyond the key in years; it's all pure jump shots now, trying for nothing but net. I recall hearing some coach years back saying that shooting off the backboard made an offensive rebound too erratic—obviated the advantage that getting inside position on your man under the basket gives you in rebounding. But back in the late 1950s, banking the ball off the board from downtown was a standard shot, nor was I the worst at it, either.

Indeed the set shot itself, not to mention the running right-hander favoured by the Celtic Bob Cousy, have also vanished from today's game. As largely has, it seems to me, the hook shot, though it hung around long enough for Kareem Abdul-Jabbar to make it—or rather the 'sky-hook'—his trademark, along with those plastic goggles. However, it wasn't the hook shot I was trying to master back in those early days—nor did I ever master it. Rather, I worked on what coaches of any sport like to call the fundamentals, the basics. Like dribbling the ball without looking at it. Which I forgot to do one Saturday afternoon when I was the only kid, luckily, on the playground, and dribbled full-speed into the iron pole holding up the basket, incurring a massive bruise just to the left of, thank God, my groin. Other fundamentals included learning to dribble with both hands, which allows you to go to your left as well as to your right. I learned to dribble with my left hand, but not well enough to use that hand under pressure from a defender. Unlike some All-Star I later read of who had dribbled a basketball to and from school each day, till he had that fundamental licked. And another who used to practice with ankle weights, so that he might leap like a kangaroo without them. I always intended to get myself a pair of ankle weights, but never did.

In sixth grade I tried out for the Russell School team. I didn't make the cut, but what hurt even worse was that Danny Brennan did. I couldn't understand that, as I felt my heart was basketball-shaped, whereas ice-hockey was Danny's first love. Besides, I had at least an inch in height on Danny. Of course the fact that he was my best friend only made it worse. I like to think seventh-grade proved me right, because that year I made the team, while Danny got cut. I warmed the bench through the regular season, but we had a strong team, which meant plenty of playing time for the subs, once the starting five had racked up enough points to put the game beyond reach.

In March the City Championships rolled around, and the Russell breezed past Houghton and their towering centre, Lou 'Bubbles' Herbert, in the semi-finals. In the finals against Putnam we led by 12-0 at the half, only to end up blowing the game. I don't remember the final score, but I do remember the scuffle in the gym lobby afterwards, in which my teammate Hank Turner pinned Putnam's Ray Rivera to the floor. Hank came out on top in that scrap, but Ray and Putnam had won the only contest that mattered that afternoon. We made the Eight-Grade City Finals the next year, only to be trounced by the Roberts School, whose skyscraper centre and future NBA starter, Billy Hewitt, was even taller than Houghton's Bubbles Herbert.

I was team manager that year, having broken my left ankle in three places playing baseball the previous summer. Danny Brennan didn't bother to try out either. But we continued to shoot hoop on the playground once I got off crutches. And we certainly continued to take in the Boston Celtics from the front row of the Boston Garden, which is a couple of rows nearer than Woody Allen ever gets to his beloved Knicks. For it happened that Danny Brennan's uncle was sportswriter Jack Barry, who covered the Celtics for *The Boston Globe*. Thus Danny and I followed the Celtics, game after game, year after year, at eye-level. We were there in the front row the afternoon the Celtics and the Minnesota Lakers lost the run of themselves, eschewing defense entirely in the highest scoring game ever: Boston 172, Minnesota 139. We were likewise there the afternoon fabled Celtic sixth-man Frank Ramsey lost his sneaker and I retrieved it, cradling it like the holy relic it was until a ball-boy took it off my hands. And not just any sneaker, mind you, but a black Converse All-Star. The Celtics were the only NBA team in black footgear, which, as Celtic coach Red Auerbach later revealed, gave every Celtic an advantage in passing off or batting a loose ball, if all he had was a below-the-knees view of surrounding players.

The Celtics were the NBA class act from the mid-Fifties through the Sixties, and once the hyper-dust has settled on the 1990s Chicago Bulls, I've no doubt the Celtics will be restored to their rightful position as the NBA Team of the Millenium. In any event, Danny and I followed them at close range, marveling at the talents of Tommy Heinsohn, or Sam Jones and KC Jones (Yes! one more), whose backcourt magic no doubt fed my own burgeoning jones. Yet most of all we marveled at Celtic 6' 10" centre Bill Russell, who was the heart and soul of the Celtics in those years, the class act of a class team. And what Russell played so brilliantly, so passionately, was defense. Nobody knew what defense Russell could play better than the late, great Wilt the Stilt (*né* Chamberlain). Wilt set an NBA record in 1962 by scoring 100 points in a single game, but basketball is a team sport, and with Russell dominating the defensive end, the Celtics were the 1962 NBA Champs (one of sixteen championship seasons), not Chamberlain's Philadelphia 76ers.

Bill Russell was the proudest athlete I've ever encountered, certainly a man of very few words. Hall of Fame Boston Red Sox slugger Ted Williams was a reserved fellah also, but you sensed Ted's silence had more to do with mere personality, whereas Russell's reserve seemed integral to his very sense of self—that of an incredibly wise, gifted and principled black man in a white man's world. Hanging out in Harvard Square on Friday night in the 1960s, Danny and I saw Bill Russell go into an apartment building on Mass Ave. We didn't move for nearly an hour, hoping to get a glimpse of him coming out. The idea of approaching Bill Russell for an autograph simply didn't occur. Other nights, hanging on the kiosk in the heart of the Square, we'd wave at Celtic Satch Sanders driving home from a game in his Mercury Cougar, and Satch would flash a smile back.

There were two public high schools in Cambridge in the early 1960s: Cambridge High & Latin School which Danny and I attended, and Rindge Technical where our far taller grade-school opponents, the aforementioned Messrs. Billy Hewitt and Bubbles Herbert had gone. Danny made the CHLS ice-hockey team, while I warmed the bench for the CHLS Freshman basketball team, and for the Junior Varsity

Home(boy) Thoughts, From Abroad

in my sophomore year, 1962, before throwing my hat at organised b-ball. As it happened, CHLS had a fair bit of talent in those years, though nothing like our sister school, Rindge Tech. Our coach was Paul Lyons, a maths teacher who had us tape our ankles even in practice, and who hung inspirational slogans in the locker room, like 'When the Going Gets Tough, the Tough Get Going'. I smiled to myself when I read years later how John Mitchell, Nixon's Attorney General and convicted Watergate conspirator, had had the same slogan on his desk. That's not to impugn Paul, of course, who had himself the utmost respect for the US Constitution. However, there was something in Paul's 90-degree, rectilinear approach that sometimes found him at odds with his more obliquely angled players. Like a kid named Jack Cadigan from East Cambridge, who had both talent and attitude. Or Beetle Jackson, who'd been two years ahead of Danny and me at the Russell School, a gifted power forward who had everything but what Coach Lyons called 'hustle'.

Brockton, home of Rocky Marciano, had a powerful high-school team in 1962, led by a Greek-American kid named George Sarantopolous, probably the best athlete to come out of that shoe-factory town since the undefeated heavyweight champ. Whether or no, Sarantopolous could drive, penetrate, and score like nobody else in the Suburban League. We played Brockton twice, once away and once at home. It was on the latter occasion that Sarantopolous elbowed our guard, Roger Dottin, a sweet skinny black kid with an amazingly idiosyncratic jump shot, in which Roger held the ball with hands either side down behind his head, before bringing it forward and releasing it overhead at the height of his jump, its trajectory describing an arc so high you feared the ball might hit the gym ceiling before it began its descent towards the basket. Roger didn't shoot much, nor did that shot always go in, either. But there was nothing more beautiful than when it found its mark, and I've never seen anybody else—playground, college or pro—ever shoot anything like it.

That afternoon, however, Roger came off the court in tears from Sarantopolous's elbow, while our entire bench seethed. Coach Lyons immediately sent in Beetle Jackson to cover Sarantopolous, and I can still see the muscles in Beetle's magnificent shoulders rippling as he loped—and there is no other word for the fluidly languid way that Beetle moved—onto the court. It happens that Beetle was, like Roger, African-American. Having said that, let me state that there had been nothing racialist about Sarantopolous or his elbow. I doubt he had even meant to hurt Roger, though I don't remember much compunction about it either. Besides, all of Roger's teammates, white and black, were equally hurt by his pain and tears. But life isn't colourblind, and none of us playing the game that afternoon were either, which at some subliminal level no doubt heightened the tension as Beetle lined up opposite Sarantopolous and play resumed. We didn't have long to wait either before the Brockton star stole the ball and raced away downcourt. Sarantopolous shot his lay-up—wearing Beetle like a second skin—and missed. No foul was called, nor had anybody, including the ref, seen anything untoward, as both players' momentum hurled them into the padded wall behind the basket. Both lads kept their feet, but while Beetle loped back down the court, Sarantopolous managed only three steps before he fell writhing to the ground, holding his rib cage, as our entire bench exhaled in unison, feeling justice to have been done.

Of course Rindge, situated just next door, were our biggest opponents. We gave them a scare in our first match, our 6' 4"

Afro-Am (and future Harvard Medical School MD) Noel Solomons playing the game of his life, but we really hadn't a chance of upsetting them that year. What's more, once the State Tourney started, all of CHLS immediately adopted the Rindge team. Games were played in the Boston Garden, and Danny Brennan and I didn't miss one, even though we hadn't our customary courtside seats. Instead we sat in the upper balcony, called by some 'Nigger Heaven', though so called, I'd warrant, by white kids who hadn't gone to primary schools like Russell or Roberts where they would have sat beside, lunched with, fought against and befriended black classmates, no different from themselves, from kindergarten on.

That year Rindge boasted *three* kids who could dunk, at a time when few high schools had a single player capable of getting the ball above the rim. Consequently Rindge's pre-game warm-up was a great crowd pleaser, climaxing in the lay-up drill which closed with reserve forward Harold Dupee, the aforementioned Billy Hewitt, and Larry Stead slamming it down in succession. Rindge that year also boasted current St John's University coach Mike Jarvis and George Hewitt in the backcourt, the latter possessed of what Celtic coach Auerbach described as the fastest hands he'd ever seen on a high-school player. Four black kids plus a Greek-American, George Anastos, whose reliable jump shot from the right corner I can see yet. All sufficient unto the night of March 12, 1962, when Rindge Tech won the Massachusetts Class A State Tourney, defeating George Sarantopolous's Brockton High 69-62 before 13,909. The game I remember well, but the exact date and capacity crowd are courtesy of a *Boston Globe* cutting Danny recently sent me, thirty-seven years after the match.

I graduated high school two years later and went on to a local college. However, Harvard had no basketball team to speak of—and certainly no roundball tradition—so I just continued to follow CHLS, Rindge and the Celtics. I played for fun sometimes with a roommate, Bo Jones, who had played his high-school ball at St Alban's in DC along with Al Gore. Bo later went off to England as a Rhodes Scholar, just like that other Ivy Leaguer, Princeton's Bill Bradley, who returned from Oxford to star for Woody Allen's New York Knicks. I went off after college to the Peace Corps, where our Puerto Rican training camp in the tropical forest above Arecibo had an outdoor court which we frequented when we weren't learning Spanish or reading about rural community development. Somewhere yet is a snapshot of myself in Puerto Rico, shooting what looks like a hook shot, though I doubt it went in. Another afternoon, fellow Volunteer Frank Censale (from Somerville High—a Massachusetts basketball powerhouse in the 1950s) and I were dropped off on a training assignment on the outskirts of the small town of Urtuado. Our assignment was to have some kind of creative engagement with the locals, and try out our still rudimentary *español*, before rendezvousing at *la plaza mayor* where we would be picked up and taken back to base. Wandering through a *barrio*, Frankie and I found a basketball court, where we promptly joined a pick-up game with a gang of local kids. Community development, how are ye!

There wasn't even a basketball hoop in the Costa Rican village near the Nicaraguan border where I spent my Peace Corps tour. However, I did secure a starting position as first-baseman for the Upala Centro baseball team, *beisbol* having been bequeathed to that region by the US Marines who had propped up a right-wing regime in Nicaragua from 1925 to

1934. There was the local football team too, but like most Americans my age, I viewed soccer as this interminable game in which twenty men chased each other around, until the end when the Germans won. I resumed playing basketball though when I returned to Massachusetts in 1970, ending up once again on crutches after a game of one-on-one with my old pal Danny Brennan at the indoor gym of the new Tobin School, which had replaced our alma mater Russell. Danny still played some ice-hockey, but worse yet he had put on a late-growing spurt and now stood 6' 7" to my 6' I could—and can—still outshoot him, but he was a bitch to shift underneath the basket, all hard angles, bony elbows and superior upper-body strength.

I went away to Ireland a few years later, which effectively ended what would otherwise have been a lifelong affair with the Boston Celtics. I did however have one more fling with a basketball team—namely the University of Massachusetts Minutemen—who were just emerging as a national collegiate power when we moved back from Ireland to Amherst, Massachusetts, in 1989, Amherst lying just nineteen miles north of Springfield, where Dr James Naismith, a Canadian-born Presbyterian minister, had hung a peach basket either end of the International YMCA Training School in December of 1890, and given us the game itself.

As it happened, my two grade-school daughters were ripe for a benign indoctrination into the joy that is roundball. And so in 1993 they proved as awestruck as I at the miraculous potential of UMass freshman centre Marcus Camby, yet another beautiful tall young black man. Meanwhile their own primary school, just behind our house, had the requisite outdoor court, which I'd occasionally visit with my own ball, noticing how it was mostly refugee Cambodian kids playing there, as if the rest of Amherst youth were indoors in front of their TVs and Nintendos. Still, in 1994 I watched my elder daughter captain her sixth-grade intramural team to the Crocker Farm School basketball championship—an upset if ever there was one. And what makes me proudest, I think, was the defense said daughter played, stuck like velcro to whomever she was marking, clogging the lane and contesting every rebound. I may not have made my own sixth-grade team, but two of my older sisters had captained their respective high school teams, and clearly the XX-linked-Glavin-basketball-gene has been handed down, most recently surfacing in my younger daughter who beat out several club players in making her own Drumcondra convent-school A team.

Such then is the stuff of a Basketball Jones: a (white) homeboy's thoughts from abroad. Though it wasn't till my video-shop encounter this summer that I realised how bereft, nay strung-out, I truly am. Reading the Irish sports-pages out of habit, but stripped of the sports, basketball and baseball, for which I lived growing up. A man without a country is a serious thing, but a man without sports is downright tragic. Not even Spike Lee's basketball film *He Got Game* (from that same northside video shop) helped fill the gap much. Though Spike's opening shot—of a *white* farm-kid shooting the ball behind his barn—is a brilliant touch, because as Spike knows, the game of basketball, unlike life, *is* colourblind, and the ball responds indiscriminately to a Larry Bird or a Magic Johnson. I managed to catch a couple of UMass's national collegiate championship play-off games on the NBC Super Channel in 1995 and '96, but I also caught *Hoop Dreams* around that time at the Irish Film Centre, a beautifully shot and heartbreaking documentary about how the Almighty Dollar—

Home(boy) Thoughts, From Abroad

which has wreaked havoc with professional sports around the globe—has by now seeped down through college programmes to poison high-school ball, not least in the US inner cities where too many black youth see basketball as their only ticket out. And, as if to underline the message, a year later we read of scandals attached to our very own beloved UMass team during those near-championship years.

Meantime, the National Basketball Association, whose so-called Dream Team ruined Olympic ball as we knew it, continues to market itself worldwide, running TV ads that show a kid bouncing a ball around the globe. You can now watch NBA ball in Ireland, but I sometimes wonder if those matches aren't just another commercial for the officially licensed NBA products which are more the point of the exercise—the spray deodorant by Faberge with its colourful NBA hologram, or Kellogg's cereal boxes emblazoned with Grant Hill and the NBA Website. Indeed, if you have the money, you can now even buy shares in the Boston Celtics or in baseball's Cleveland Indians. So while I may watch some NBA ball on telly this winter, I probably won't watch much. On the other hand, if former Princeton, NY Knick and US Senator Bill Bradley gets as far as the Massachusetts Democratic primary, he'll get my absentee ballot, because no (Anglo) US politician speaks as eloquently about the need to heal America's racial divide as Bradley, who witnessed the discrimination that his teammates of colour had to endure off the court.

And I'll surely go to the Dublin City University gym again this year, lace up my sneakers (black Converse All-Stars, natch!), and continue to work on my turn-around jump shot. And going to my left. My bones are too old to risk a pick-up game, though sometimes I watch from the balcony, marveling how these white Irish kids, both guys and dolls, can run, cut, fake, dish, and shoot with the best of them. Watching them, I feel that basketball will do just fine, despite the money, marketing and hype. Because all it takes is a hoop, a ball and some kind of level surface. And even two kids can play: One-on-One, Twenty-One, or H-O-R-S-E. Or just one kid, playing One-on-None, as I did for hours on that long-ago Russell playground. Nowadays TV ads use basketball to flog Snickers to kids worldwide, but those same kids, like the Cambodians of Amherst, can still encounter the game itself on its own terms. Which is to say: always follow through on your shot, keep yourself between your man (or woman) and the basket, and never cross your legs while defending. For sure basketball will survive as a game, no matter how it prospers as a sport. And any youngsters who strive to dribble with both hands are still likely to learn something about passion, grace, geography, memory, not to mention brotherhood.

A few weeks after spotting the Big Fellah in the video shop this summer, I visited a friend in Spain, whose son has a gigantic poster of Michael Jordan in his bedroom, taking a rebound away from his own teammate Dennis Rodman (who only played to rebound), and believe it or not, from my old CHLS teammate, Patrick Ewing. A poster which, nicely enough, allows me to tie up a couple of loose ends. The first being Michael Jordan. How can I possibly, you might ask, write an essay on *baloncesto* without mentioning former Chicago White Sox minor-league outfielder Michael Jordan till the very end? The answer is simple: what hasn't already been said about His Airness? Only this: check out Michael's number. Twenty-three, which he even had embossed on his silk dress shirts. Look it up under Occult, or talk to a numerologist friend, and you'll discover there exists a body of lore concerning the magical properties of that particular number. Hermann Hesse knew about it, among others. Laugh if you like, but how else can you begin to explain what Jordan could do on—and off—the ball?

The other loose end is my old teammate Patrick. Truth be told, there were more than a few years between us in high school, and by the time Patrick suited up, Cambridge High & Latin and Rindge Tech had amalgamated into Cambridge Rindge & Latin, which Patrick led to the Massachusetts State Championship titles in 1979 and 1980. Yet what I claimed still holds—that Patrick and I once played for the same high school team. And that's a helluva lot closer to the real thing than Woody Allen will ever get.

Basketball Jones, I got a Basketball Jones
Got a Basketball Jones, oh baby, oo-oo-ooo...

THE END OF THE ROAD
Jim Lusby

Named after the French expression for 'the grace of God', the road was crowded with working people to whom a foreign language and a helpful deity were equally distant realities. The descent away from it towards Waterford's steamier bars and ballrooms was predictably all downhill, but the steep and thorny climb in the opposite direction unfairly led only to Gallows Hill. Its tiny houses were too cramped to contain anything except the family arguments and its front doorsteps led directly to the street, but the back gardens seemed to stretch away forever from the small yards and into private dreams.

In the late Fifties and early Sixties, when I was growing up on Gracedieu Road, most of those dreams seemed to be carried on the hunched shoulders and bobbing heads of racing greyhounds.

There are always exceptions, of course. Eight doors down from us, for instance, lived the only man I ever knew whose children dreamed of opening the batting for Ireland. One long and tiresome winter, he laid an entire cricket pitch in his garden. With wooden laths and wire mesh, he enclosed it in home-made practice nets; and then he spent all the following summer dispatching my tame outswingers with such unerring accuracy that he eventually drove the ball through a weakened section of the wire and into the next garden, where his eighty-six-year-old neighbour, fielding patiently at cover point for three-and-a-half months, gleefully snapped it up and impounded it as booty from the boundary war between the houses. Further away, an old Protestant lady whose merchant family had declined in the Irish Free State now entertained confused grandchildren on a cramped croquet lawn; and nearer home again, a rough tennis court once made a brief appearance.

But these were unusual. For most working people, it was the greyhounds that held the promise of everything their ordinary lives denied them.

Bought or adopted as a newly-weaned pup, the dog was a personal investment in a different kind of future. Owned, trained, housed and groomed by one man, it offered the illusion of total mastery to conceal the grim reality of slavery, a trick the working man mistakenly blamed his wife for inventing. And on race nights, for thirty intense seconds around the oval track at Kilcohan Park, while its owner watched from the stand, with his heart in his mouth and his money safely tucked away in the bookmaker's bag, there was a hectic drama of the ordinary man's own creating, to which he had contributed an essential ingredient. Almost uniquely, greyhound racing seemed to offer no distinctions between spectator and participant.

But this was probably as much a feature of the times as of the sport, before the dominance of television tempted us to sit in front of a flickering screen all day and be assured of missing nothing, except living itself. The road, for instance, traditionally fed the Mount Sion hurling club and the schoolboy soccer clubs of Bohemians and Crusaders and through them the county hurling and city soccer teams. So standing on the terraces at Walsh Park, while the hurlers played host to Tipperary in a championship clash, or at Kilcohan Park for a League of Ireland decider against Dundalk or Shamrock Rovers, was never all that far away, or all that much different, from the street games we played with plastic footballs between goalposts made of sweaters. The gap was measured in hours, not status. Today's heroes had played here yesterday; tomorrow we might join them ...

There was a sense of continuity about it all, a feeling of wholeness. A unity that started to fracture, I think, in the mid-Sixties, when the goalkeeper Peter Thomas and the left winger Johnny Matthews, both from Coventry, the Derry midfielder Jimmy McGeough and others from outside the city, were all signed by the Waterford soccer team, forming the core of a brilliant squad that would go on to win six League of Ireland championships in the following years, while young Waterford players, forgotten in the flush of local pride that came with such heady success, drifted into junior football or out of the sport completely. And significantly, it was also around this time that the gardens on the road were re-designed and newly devoted to rhododendron, or iceberg lettuce, or prize-winning squashes, or even, in one or two advanced cases, to medium-grade cannabis plants that were grown under plastic greenhouses, dried out on the slate roofs and smoked in front of the recently installed tile fireplaces. A modern ambivalence had replaced the old-fashioned confusion on the road.

We had no greyhounds of our own at home. To my shame, my placid, taciturn father, a Protestant married into a Roman Catholic community, preferred to keep his head down with the more solitary business of breeding prize chaffinches inside the house and rearing chickens in the back garden. It was my mother's two brothers, living only seven doors away from us, but still occupying alien territory as far as my father was concerned, who kept the dogs.

From the beginning, my attitude to greyhounds was hopelessly divided. On the one hand, they were noble hounds, romantically linked with the wild and with Celtic superheroes, infinitely superior to the fairly limited, and fairly boring, farmyard fowl whose only contributions to the English language were the insults hen-pecked, mother-hen, and chicken. On the other, the dogs were staunch Roman Catholics, invariably blessed as pups by the local curate, and so representative of everything the heroic had been shrivelled to in late-fifties Ireland, of a narrow conservatism that made my father's solitary hobbies look at times like reckless individualism.

There was also a more personal loss that the dogs were responsible for. Visiting my relatives one September Sunday morning—apparently to observe the weekly courtesy due my aunt and two uncles, but in reality to plunder again the black and red currants, the raspberries and wild strawberries that grew in abundance in their back yard—I found that all the fruit plants had just been brutally uprooted, found the bushes lying withering and the berries already rotting, and the corpses strewn around the fresh foundations of what would eventually become extensive dog kennels and paddocks. It was the end of innocence. For after years of fiddling around with one or two witless, talentless mutts, my uncles were now seriously into greyhounds.

More than the fruit suffered, of course, in that initial drive.

At the time, my uncles were big, working men, slaughterers and boners in Denny's bacon factory nearby, with their hob-nailed boots firmly stuck in the conventions of their generation. In ordinary circumstances, if their sister was somehow unavailable, both would've eaten raw meat before either starving or cooking. Neither Big-Endians or Little-Endians, these rough bachelors had made a political statement out of their inability to boil an egg, a manifesto out of their refusal to learn.

And now?

Now they not only collected sheeps' heads from local butchers and brought them home, but they spent hours afterwards boiling the skulls, popping the cooked eyeballs from their sockets and shredding the meat from the bones, until a sweetish smell of overcooked organs started to cling to their house and to their own clothes. They brought a heavy iron mincer, clamped it to the kitchen table, and used it to grind cheap but nutritious cuts of beef. From a local wholesaler, they ordered huge bags of meal, mixing the grain with the raw and cooked meats to form the basis of the dogs' diet. Until finally, standing one freezing February morning in the middle of all these riches and looking out the kitchen window on the completed paddocks in the back garden, it suddenly occurred to me. The dogs were eating better than I was! In at least one respect, and probably in others, the dogs' life was superior to my own.

There were other revolutions.

Like most men of their time, my uncles' attention to personal grooming was fairly restricted. There was the obsessive polishing of their footwear, a quaint neurosis that seemed to concern Irish mothers of the period. And there was the vain brushing of their slicked-back hair, an image copied from the contemporary rebels, Elvis Presley and James Dean. But between these contradictory extremes, their neglected bodies were largely untroubled by fussing.

Things were different with the greyhounds. Long hours

were punched in keeping a dog's coat clean and free of loose hairs, on the understanding that the laws of aerodynamics would reward your diligence on race nights. The animal's toes were frequently clipped and filed, to reduce the risk of injury while racing. And its muscles were constantly toned with oils and hand massage.

The current assumption, again from the dominance of television, is that sport is the opium of the masses, that essentially it involves a lonely fan's strange identification with a distant club which imports strangers and pays them outrageous multiples of the fan's own meagre income. This unhealthy mix of resentment and dependence is not something my uncles would've admired. In all my childhood, I can remember only one such fan on the road. Married, but embittered, he hung panting around his disdainful wife, like a dog trailing a bitch in heat, because he occasionally needed sex. And he was known as The Ghost.

Years after I left behind my uncles' immersion in their sport, I read Peter Handke's novel *The Goalie's Anxiety at the Penalty Kick* and I consciously recognized, probably for the first time, how much of a unity their lives had been. In the story, Joseph Bloch, a former goalkeeper, suddenly drops out of daily life and then kills a woman for no apparent reason. At the end of the novel, he's watching a soccer match. But he doesn't follow the movement of the ball or the progress of the game; he watches the goalkeeper running around the penalty area without the ball. You get used to it, he claims, but it's ridiculous.

Sport, in other words, has no power to correct a warp, because it's not distinct from the rest of life. With its accepted rules, its limited playing area and its conclusive winners and losers, it's obviously less complicated than anything else. But apart from this absorbing simplicity, it has no claims to superiority.

And so, as one decade gave way to another and as our self-contained, insular little world felt the first, disturbing touches of the more open Sixties, my own attitude to the dogs, just like my attitude to most things on the road, remained ambivalent.

Not that there wasn't plenty to enthral a boy in dog racing.

Like spies and secret agents, racing greyhounds lead double lives and have two names. Mid-week, they could be warm, frisky companions, named Rosie, or Jack. But Saturday night, placed into traps on the racing track, crouching there in anticipation of the approaching hare and that mad hurtle against five other dogs to the first bend, they were pure professionals again, cold and focused, and appropriately named, as Bilberry Blue, or Lightening Lad.

And just as in the murky worlds of Graham Greene and John le Carré, affection always betrayed you.

I remember a much-loved brindle bitch who had broken her toes too often to retain the hope of racing and who wasn't considered good enough to breed from. I remember walking her, past Gallows Hill, and out to the local abattoir, where a fat man in a blood-soaked apron took her from me. And I remember standing outside, looking in through the open door, while he held a gun to her head and drove a bolt through her brain.

When the fat man came back, he gave me the empty lead and leather collar; and as I carried the equipment home, I felt a ghost tugging on it all the way. It would've been better, for me, if I'd left home with two greyhounds, keeping one for company on the way back. But such were the priorities of dedicated sportspeople, that this was considered too unsettling for the surviving dog.

The End of the Road

There were other, less traumatic, involvements. This was where I first came across the controversy about doping in sport, for instance, thirty years before it publicly tainted the Olympic Games. And where I first brushed with fraud, and fixing, and sabotage.

Greyhound racing is about gambling as much as about play. And where there is money, there are always scams. Dogs held back by being over-fed before races and then slimmed down to romp home—theoretically, anyway—at generous odds. Dogs stuffed with magic pills that were meant to make them stronger, faster, fitter, but more often only made the dim-witted goofier and the sluggish more like snails. Time trials rigged, so that a promising puppy went into its first competitive race showing a vital tenth of a second slower over the 525 yards than he'd actually run.

And yet ...

Despite the cloak and dagger, despite the heavy investment, there was still the sense of something unsatisfying, of something missing. It wasn't always, or very often, all that exciting. Like every sport, greyhound racing is mostly dedicated preparation. Mostly slog. The long daily walks in all weathers to build up a dog's stamina. The uphill gallops to increase its strength. The careful diet to keep its weight steady.

And the more specialised training.

On the oval track, there are two crucial sections to a race. One is the break from the traps. If a dog breaks poorly, is easily distracted or turns inside the traps, it almost invariably struggles. If it breaks well, it gains an advantage that is difficult to drag back. The second, equally vital, element is the first bend, when six dogs converge at 40 m.p.h. on a space that's too narrow to contain more than one or two of them, and where a bump, or a grind, or a crash can finish a dog's race, or a dog's career.

Almost all races on the track were lost and won between the traps and that first bend. Every greyhound owner already knows this, but the hard work is sharing the knowledge with the greyhounds themselves.

Hard work. Repetitious. And humdrum. And to justify it, you need the intoxication, the forgetfulness, of victory. If not the ultimate high of national glory, then at least enough local fame to nurture hope, to keep you going.

But for my uncles and myself, success remained as elusive as ever. We had the occasional dog of promise, the occasional win in small races at Kilcohan Park; but it was always followed by a string of defeats once the dog moved up in class. And we never got anywhere near the peaks of the racing calendar, the Derby and the Oaks in Dublin's Shelbourne Park.

Maybe I was losing in the dogs. Maybe the golden age of greyhound racing as the working man's sport was already past. Maybe I didn't have my uncles' powers of involvement. Or maybe I was on the verge of other things. Secondary school. Organized schoolboy football. More attractive models: in my brother's soccer team, Crusaders, who were under-15 national champions, and in the Waterford hurling team, which captured the All-Ireland title the same year.

But the dogs weren't quite ready to let me go yet.

When glory came, though, it wasn't on the track, which I was familiar with, but in the shadowy world of open coursing, which I hadn't yet been initiated into. A man's world, as I was often warned. What the phrase meant, I had no idea. I had only the sensation of an exasperating barrier, beyond which I couldn't follow my uncles any more.

The End of the Road

Now and again, I caught brief glimpses of the forbidden. After vanishing mysteriously for days, leaving the remaining dogs in the dubious care of my aunts, my mother and myself, my uncles would suddenly turn up again in muddied wellingtons, rough and unshaven, smelling of stale booze and sweat and of the ditch where they'd slept the previous night, with the greyhound they'd brought with them either preening and pampered in front after a successful campaign or else dragged along behind, limp with the shame of its own failure.

But they were also storytellers, my uncles; great enhancers of life with words. All that family were. It was a talent my mother used against my father's silences, lobbing words of varying sharpness at him, like an artillery battery trying to find its range, until something finally hit home and exploded. So right through that long winter of our glory, as the massive fawn dog I knew as Prince coursed across Munster, working his way to the culminating final of the season, I missed nothing of his exploits except their immediacy, and gained as much in the retelling as the victories themselves did.

I wasn't meant to go to that final. My mother disapproved of coursing. But between the first refusal and the Sunday of the final, something shifted in the unstable world of my parents' relationship. Maybe my father was pleased that I wasn't going. Maybe he had another treat in store for me. And maybe his plans helped change my mother's mind. I don't know. I never discovered. But I suspect that sport is *always* political.

Sunday morning, in a black Austin A35 from which I watched the tarmacadam whizzing by through the holes in the corroded chassis, I travelled with a huddle of supporters from the road. Inevitably, once we were outside the county, past the last of the familiar pubs we needed to stop at, we got lost on the signpost-less rural roads. I still have no idea where we finally ended up. Somewhere in South Tipperary, I believe.

Already late, we abandoned the car by the side of the road, climbed a ditch and trudged across the open fields, until we reached the source of the cheering we had heard. What we came on was a magnificent arena. Without grandstands. Without terraces. Without even a marked playing area. But an arena nonetheless.

Two colourful lines of densely crowded spectators flanked a wide central aisle in the muddy field. As we hurried to join them, they were busy and boisterous. Arguing the odds. Placing their bets. Shouting scorn and encouragement. We searched for information. Picked up garbled snatches. Fitted the pieces together. For an hour, it seemed, the last two dogs had raced to near exhaustion, matching each other point for point, stride for stride. Now the last, decisive race was about to start.

And then the crowd fell suddenly silent. Tense. Expectant. At the end of the field, the slipper held the two straining greyhounds, our own fawn warrior and a huge black beast that looked even meaner, and more imposing, and surely unbeatable. Behind them, a line of beaters fanned the next field, flushing out the hare and driving it to run the gauntlet past the dogs and between the lined spectators.

A strange cheer went up as the confused little animal scuttled into the arena. A strangled cheer, more of anticipation than involvement. Because the hare was incidental to the main business. And no one bothered with its progress once it passed.

Or no one except myself. Pushed to the front of the crowd—one of the few privileges always granted children—I was immediately fascinated by this lonely creature, this unpredictable mover that was so unlike the mechanical hare on the oval track, this strange nonentity that was at once expendable and indispensable. Like Joseph Bloch watching the unoccupied goalie keeping warm, I missed the point of the game and only afterwards, when the victory was cold, learned that our fawn Prince broke poorly from the slipper, looked beaten almost immediately, but then miraculously recovered, paying back all those tedious hours spent walking and galloping him, and was the first to turn the hare and shade the contest over his opponent.

I saw none of it. I heard the wild shouts of triumph at the conclusion, and although it was my first experience of men so utterly lost in celebration, I couldn't join them. For me, it wasn't over.

As Prince turned his quarry, the hare twisted back, into the path of the onrushing black greyhound. It sprang off its powerful hind legs to evade this new danger, contorting itself in mid-air. But it was too late. Simultaneously, its neck and hind legs were grabbed by the separate jaws of the greyhounds. And as both dogs instinctively shook it, the animal was ripped in two.

I didn't know then what I felt at this spectacle. I wasn't squeamish. I had no pity for the hare. I wasn't disgusted. Even then, I knew that the spectators weren't cheering the death of the hare, but only the victory of one dog over another. They would've preferred if the hare had escaped to course another day, but they were otherwise indifferent to it.

It was only later that I clarified my own response. And in slow stages. At a boxing match in one of Waterford's gyms, when a senseless, bloodied fighter lay defeated on the canvas, ignored by everyone except his trainer and his distraught girl friend. At a savage contest between two snarling pit bull terriers and at another between two fighting cocks armed with sharpened steel talons. Reminders that sport can still so easily slip back over that hazy, uncertain line, into its brutal origins in the hunt and the chase and the kill. Just as it can also topple forwards, over that increasingly obscured line that divides it from commerce. That the path it holds to is narrow and precarious.

There are no dogs any more in my uncles' back garden in Waterford. Because there are no uncles any more. One was stricken by diabetes in his thirties. In the worst of the working man's stubborn traditions, he refused to have it properly diagnosed and contained. Within a year, he was blind and incapacitated. Within another, he had lost everything to the illness, including his natural gift for narrative. He still talked, but since he was confined to the house now, with no new sights to nourish his descriptions and no new experiences to vary his tales, his stories became repetitious, redundant, irrelevant, tedious. The other uncle kept pace with life, kept breeding and training greyhounds, but still died of heart failure before his elder, ailing brother.

The dog kennels they built are all ruins now. The roofs have caved in. The brick walls are crumbling. The debris is overgrown with weeds. And among them, if you look very closely, you can see the tangle of an old red current bush, resiliently reclaiming the ground that was taken from it almost forty years ago.

The trophies won by my uncles' dogs lie on a dark mahogany sideboard inside the now deserted house. Neglected. Covered with dust. Underneath each, if it was lifted, there must be a little circle of brightness, from when the bases were proudly laid on the polished surface. Better not to expose these windows to decay, of course. Better to imagine the men and dogs still living beyond them. And still striving. Still involved.

WINNER ALL RIGHT
Anthony Cronin

A foreign dignitary on a visit to England was asked if he would like to see the Derby. He replied that it was a fact already known to him that one horse could run faster than another over a given distance; and that he saw no reason why he should subject himself to the noise and bustle of a huge crowd of people on a hot day in order to verify it. He may have been something of a philosopher, but like many philosophers, he was also a bit of a fool.

Trivial pursuits are a major part of human existence, perhaps even the best part. Samuel Johnson, also something of a philosopher, was nearer to the truth than that foreign dignitary when he said that the great art of happiness consisted in being interested in things that are of no philosophical consequence. The other, he said, give us misery to no end.

'The lure of the turf' is a rather lurid phrase, familiar to readers of moralistic Victorian novels and suggesting the ruin of ancient houses and family fortunes gone into the coffers of wicked bookmakers. Yet in the long and troubled history of mankind, it would surely be difficult to find another activity that has given so much pleasure to so many people so consistently as horse-racing has.

There was a race at the Curragh of Kildare in pre-historic times. There is a stretch of turf on the Derby course at Epsom that is said to be greener than its surroundings because of the number of people who have had their ashes scattered there. For many intelligent and reasonable people horse-racing has a deep and powerful attraction that goes far beyond its apparent deserts.

The idea that backing horses is all about gambling is fallacious. Gambling has its own romance and part of the fascination of the turf used to be that people were either made or ruined by it. It develops certain qualities in people usually thought desirable—decisiveness, optimism, nerve. But though most of those who go racing like to have a bet, they can scarcely be called gamblers, any more than people who play spoil five for shillings or pence.

Edgar Wallace said that the mind must be in a state of complete equipoise before it is safe to back horses. A man who has had a row with his wife that morning, he insisted, should not go to a racecourse. Making up your mind what to back is a very difficult and delicate activity. So difficult is it sometimes that, unless there is a documented bet, you cannot be sure what you would actually have backed or what has been your selection. Besides being a commercial transaction with a hope of gain, the bet is an expression of conviction and a record of commitment.

Of course most people who are interested in racing do like to play the odds; but they also liked to be proved right—that is to say, to win—irrespective of the amount staked or won. One of the main joys of the process is that you can actually see your win evolve before your eyes. It is not like simply turning a blind card face up. And if there is anything better than watching your horse come with a long sustained run on the rails, it is watching him take a commanding lead early and keep it all the way. Patrick Kavanagh, a devoted punter and racegoer, once backed a horse at the Phoenix Park which led all the way and was fifteen lengths clear at the finish. He said it was the most exciting finish he had ever seen.

But perhaps the best way to illustrate the thrill of backing a winner is to take an example from another discipline. In 1905, Einstein published the Special Theory of Relativity, the result of much cogitation and calculation. Naturally his theory was disputed, but he had made a prediction. When four years later, an eclipse of the sun would enable the path of light from the planet Mercury to be observed accurately, he would, he said, be shown to have been right. In 1909, this future event took place. Einstein was right.

It is not too much to say that when one backs a winner, especially of a race to which one has been able to give time and thought, one feels a little like Einstein felt on that memorable occasion. Most people who back horses do give time and thought to the matter and they reach theoretical conclusions on the probable outcome of certain races which may or may not be justified by the actuality. When the race is run and the result comes in, or, to use an old racing phrase, when the numbers go into the frame, you are proved beyond dispute to have been either right or wrong. And there are not many other things in the world about which one is ever proved to have been unambiguously and indisputably right— or, for that matter, unambiguously and indisputably wrong. And of course sometimes you win a little money, which can be a matter of great satisfaction. And sometimes the money is needed and that is better still.

The English Derby is run at Epsom Downs in Surrey, about fifteen miles from the centre of London and it has been run there over almost the same stretch of ground for 216 years. There was a time when reference to 'the Epsom Derby' was regarded as *lèse majesté*. There was only one Derby. It was the other races, whether in France or Ireland or the United States, which had to have a geographical prefix, being only the Irish Derby or the French Derby or the Kentucky Derby or whatever. The real Derby was run at Epsom and the day on which it was run was 'Derby Day', with both houses of Parliament adjourned, much ordinary business suspended and a vast concourse of people assembling at Epsom Downs.

But it is precisely the fact that it is run at Epsom which is now a key cause of controversy. The mile-and-a-half course there is not so much a switch-back as a roller-coaster, entirely unsuited to three-year-old thoroughbreds at the stage of their development at which they are called upon to race there. The hill down to Tattenham Corner is the steepest on any English racecourse except Brighton (or any Irish racecourse except humble Tramore). At the corner, the ground falls alarmingly away from the rails, a camber which has no sooner been adjusted to than it tilts up and goes the other way, sloping in towards the rails in the final, steep uphill stages.

In the old days, people used to speak about Epsom approvingly as 'the supreme test of a thoroughbred'. And test it certainly is. Not only a horse's speed and stamina, but its courage and confirmation, are put to the proof there. Once upon a time, the runners had to walk across the Downs through all the vast and noisy crowd—far vaster and noisier than any of them were likely to have seen before—to get to the mile-and-a-half start. Many good horses were in such a lather of sweat before the race began that their chance was virtually gone. Nowadays they canter down the racecourse to get to the starting gate and the test of temperament is less severe and searching. But it still takes a pretty cool customer to get through the preliminaries, including the parade in front of the stands, without boiling over. And this is as it should be. A horse's temperament is an important part of its general ability.

In the race itself the runners are required to gallop at full stretch up hill and down dale for a mile-and-a-half, a distance over which most of them have never been tried before; to gallop against the collar for the first four furlongs and against—as you might say—the grain for the next four, before encountering the tricky finishing straight, with its demands on stamina and its final deep inclination towards the inside rail which makes it difficult to keep balanced.

The first bend of the Derby course, encountered while the runners are still travelling uphill, is to the right; the second to the left. Because it is so easy to get chopped off at either of these bends, a fierce pace is usually set; and the fact that there is constant jockeying for position coming down the hill, when a number of horses who have reached the limit of their stamina are falling back, ensures that the Derby is, more often than not, a very rough race.

The Derby tests speed, stamina and temperament all at once as no other race does; but we have, alas, now moved into an era when most owners and trainers do not want their horses to be tested to the full in all departments, particularly where there are risks involved. For most of them the main object of owning a very expensive thoroughbred is to acquire a reputation for it as easily, quickly and safely as possible and then pack it off for a highly profitable career at stud. Critics of the Derby say that it comes too early in the season, when most of the runners are not fully mature and that racing at full stretch over the Epsom mile-and-a-half involves an unjustifiable amount of risk to a horse's delicate limbs and general well-being. But one cannot help feeling that much of the criticism which is now being voiced is based on financial considerations. To run a horse in the Derby, against the very best of its contemporaries, is to risk more than injury. It is to risk exposing your horse's limitations in a pretty thoroughgoing way.

The first Epsom Derby I ever saw featured the Aga Khan's Tulyar in 1952. He was trained by Marcus Marsh and ridden in the great race by Charlie Smirke, otherwise known as 'cheerful Charlie'. Smirke was a Cockney from London's East End who had no racing background. When he retired from the saddle he severed all connection with racing. At this point he had had a chequered career which included lengthy absences due to suspensions by the racing authorities which many thought unjust and service in the war. But he had already ridden three Derby winners and it was said of him that he knew every blade of grass on the Epsom course.

Tulyar was not a very good two-year-old and had not figured in the winter betting for the Derby. But early in his three-year-old season he beat a very fast horse called King's Bench over seven furlongs, virtually at sprint distance, at Hurst Park. When King's Bench went on to run second in the Two Thousand Guineas, the first classic of the season, run over a mile at Newmarket, it began to seem to me at least that the Aga Khan's horse might have a chance in the Derby. And when he confirmed his stamina by winning the Ormonde Stakes at Chester, which is a mile and seven furlong race, and then went on to win the Lingfield Derby Trial, which is run over the Derby distance of a mile and a half, I began to take that chance seriously, for it now appeared that he had both speed and stamina, the two main desiderata for a Derby candidate. But the racing press was not interested and neither, it seemed, was the betting public, for a few days beforehand the bookmakers were offering the very generous odds of 100-6 on his chances. This may have been because of his poor form the previous season or because, in what was generally a warm, dry summer, his trainer said several times that he thought the horse needed soft ground such as he had got at Chester and Hurst Park. It was probably also due to the dominance of French horses at the time. One of them, Thunderhead, had won the Two Thousand Guineas; and another, Faubourg, who had cracking form in France, was favourite for the big race.

I was in London at the time and to say that I had no money would be to give a false impression. I had, if that is possible, a negative amount of money and I was getting pretty desperate. I had an account with a bookmaker, so that I could bet on credit, but I was unfortunately over the agreed limit and it was questionable whether any more of my bets would be taken. I had noticed Tulyar's seeming combination of speed and stamina after the Ormonde Stakes and though everybody I spoke to was scornful of his chances, I had begun to think that he was the Derby winner. After he won the Lingfield Trial I had begun to think he was something of a certainty.

In those days, cash betting was illegal in England but you could post cash to a Scottish bookmaking firm and have a bet that way, provided the envelope was postmarked before the time of the race. There was a famous firm called McLean's in Glasgow which advertised winnings by return. Their advertisement said postal or money orders, but what if one posted them a cheque? I had a bank account which, like my account with the bookmakers, was overdrawn. But I worked out that if one posted them a cheque for £12 to arrive on the morning of the race and they dispatched the winnings immediately I would be able to put their cheque in the bank to cover my own.

This I did; and if all went well I now stood to win £200, an enormous sum for me—and for many people—in those days, more than you would get as an advance on a novel, particularly a first novel—not that I had any intention of writing a novel. But, on the morning of the race, I took my courage in my hands and rang the bookmaking firm to whom I owed money. The kind person who took the bet seemed to have no objection to my having another £10 on at starting price, so, if McLean's did as I hoped, I now stood to win upwards of £300.

There was a huge crowd at Epsom, more people than I thought I had ever seen gathered in one place before, and the atmosphere was a jolly one, with that great Cockney specialty, jellied eels, seemingly in good supply on the outside and champagne already being drunk in the bar I was in. In those far-off days, the traditional fair was in the centre of the course and it was a much more raucous and raffish affair than the sanitised version which, in this puritanical age, takes place at the top of the hill. To a connoisseur of low life, such as I was then, the fair, with its sideshows, curiosities, beer tents and boxing booths was a pleasure in itself. But on this particular occasion I was intent on something else.

I watched the race from what was then called the Old Stewards stand, an open-topped affair which was on the outside but right on the winning post. I could not see the bookmakers from where I was wedged in, but there was a tic tac man perched on the wall near me energetically using the peculiar code—something like the deaf alphabet—which was employed in those days to signal bets from bookmakers in one ring to another. In the last few minutes before the race his hands in their white gloves were working frenetically, and when I called out to him to ask what was being backed he told me it was 'all bleeding Tulyar' and that he was now favourite at 11-2. I was watching a considerable proportion of my winnings disappear before my eyes.

It was a beautiful summer day at Epsom and the fine weather had lasted for several days, which meant that the going was firm. I did not know it then, but when the horse had had his final gallop a few days beforehand Smirke had been told to bring him up a peat moss strip on the gallops. Instead, to his trainer's horror, he brought him up a parallel strip where the ground was as hard as an airport runway and when he got down afterwards reported that there was nothing to worry about because Tulyar was even better on top of the ground than he was on the soft. It was armed with this news that his owner's son, the celebrated playboy Prince Aly Khan, who had recently married Rita Hayworth, had stepped in and had £40,000 on the horse, which, like my own poor bet, was, relatively speaking, a huge sum for those days, enough to invest and live comfortably on while you wrote poetry or novels or whatever you pleased. And not only was the Aly Khan backing his father's horse, but Smirke, it seemed, had given an interview in which he said that after the race he would be saying 'I Tulyar so'. This piece of ghastly Cockney phonetics had, according to next day's papers caused 'every housewife in England' to back his mount—illegally, of course, but the money got back to the course just the same.

When the horses paraded in front of the stands, Tulyar seemed small but every inch a racehorse; and Smirke sat on him with a half-smile, looking about him with an air of supreme confidence which suggested that the widespreading Downs and the Derby with all its great traditions belonged to him that day—as, in a sense, they did. I have never been so certain that any horse was going to win any race as I was at that moment.

In 1952, they still lined up behind a tape for the start of the great race, but they got away evenly enough and at the top of the hill a horse called Monarch More led them at a good pace, with Chavey Down, Thunderhead, Faubourg and Tulyar in close attendance. There was little change in the order until they turned for home where Chavey Down briefly took over from a beaten Monarch More, but I could see that Smirke was only biding his time and when he took up the running two furlongs out and went a couple of lengths clear I was sure it was all over. Then, an outsider, Gay Time, ridden by a young jockey named Lester Piggott, threw down a persistent and, for a moment or two, dangerous-seeming challenge. But Smirke never went for his whip and as they passed the post he was three-quarters of a length to the good with, it seemed to me, a fair bit in hand. I had (I hoped) won about £250 and I had been proved right, braving a good deal of authoritative contrary opinion in the process.

But there was drama still to follow, with, for a very long time, no sign of the "winner all right" flag going up on the number board and rumours sweeping the racecourse. It eventually transpired that Gay Time's jockey had been unseated shortly after passing the post and that the horse had gone for another little gallop on his own on the part of the Downs called The Durdans, all this taking place out of sight of most of the huge crowd. Since there was no public address system then, the wildest notions about the reasons for the delay in announcing the winner could flourish. What we didn't know until later was that the callow and inexperienced Lester Piggott had wanted to object to the winner on the grounds that Smirke had 'leaned on him' all the way up the straight. Fortunately the owner and trainer of Gay Time had dissuaded him and when at long last his saddle had been recovered and he was able to weigh in, Tulyar was deservedly announced the winner in the ordinary way.

The Aga Khan's little brown colt, who was a May foal and therefore less mature than most of his contemporaries, went on to win several big races that season, in fact almost every one he could conceivably run in, including the Eclipse Stakes, the King George the Fifth and Queen Elizabeth Stakes at Ascot and, finally, the last classic of the season, the St Leger. Thus, like many other champions of the past, he disproved the now fashionable theory that the Derby does lasting damage to immature three-year-olds. At the end of the season he was bought by the Irish Government for breeding purposes for the then unheard of sum of £250,000. There was an acrimonious debate in Dail Eireann about such a huge expenditure and during it the jockey Michael Beary, an Irishman who had been at the top of his profession in England for two or three decades, sent the Dail a telegram saying, 'Congratulations. You have bought the best horse in the world from five furlongs to five miles.'

But this sort of high finance was not my concern as I anxiously waited for McLean's cheque the following day. When it arrived I did the decent thing, putting it straight into the bank so that those good people in Glasgow would not be at the loss of the original £12. I am afraid the balance did not last as long as it might have; but I had the consolation of having been proved right about a seemingly imponderable future event, a considerable pleasure in itself, almost comparable to Einstein's in 1909. And disproportionate though all the fuss—the column inches, the cheering, the huge crowd—might seem to some, as far as a large and, I think, sensible part of humanity was concerned, I had seen history made on Epsom Downs.

THE BUTTERFLY AND THE BABY
Ulick O'Connor

I was coming back from Chicago after a television show. As I got on the plane I saw a man through the glass panel of the first-class cabin. It was like someone I'd seen a long time ago—the young Cassius Clay. It couldn't be, but it was—the butterfly himself.

'Lo,' said Muhammad Ali.

'Hello,' I said.

'This is a poet,' he explained to his travelling companion, a black gentleman with a broken nose (my *Lifestyles* had been published recently).

Ali said he'd come down to my seat in a while. I was surprised when he did, fifteen minutes later. He wanted to talk 'poetry'. I showed him a book of my poems. He inspected it with care, placing an enormous thumb and finger on the pages to span alternate lines.

'I like these 'cos they rhyme,' he announced finally. Then he began to recite his own verse, declaiming it in a sing-song Southern accent, looking ahead, but watching carefully out of the corner of his eye to see how I was reacting.

I mean—what do you do when you're sitting crouched under a mammoth who put Sonny Liston away in Round Two?

It's not exactly the place to tell him his poems don't work. But in fact here and there were lines which could stand on their own—even if they weren't written by a heavyweight champ.

> *The same road that connects*
> *two souls together*
> *When stretched becomes a*
> *path to God.*

Or:

> *When the ears of the heart*
> *Can sense the ears of other hearts*
> *Words become unnecessary.*

Ali kept his poetry recital going for an hour. Sitting in the next seat, I was able to have a close-up view of his face—unlined despite punches that would have left another man's face like Limerick lace. His ears are close to his head, neat and well-formed. Long fingers, powerful, but with a touch of elegance. When he straightens up in his seat you can see his trousers stretched tightly over gigantic thighs which are more than two feet in circumference.

I asked him how he could remember so much of his own verse.

'When I go up to Pennsylvania to work out and give up eating pork [this is because of his Muslim beliefs] I just fill up with words.'

This was 1974, before the Foreman fight. He told me calmly that he would beat Foreman—no bombast now. (We were, after all, fellow poets.) He felt Foreman could not hit him.

'I roll with every punch. Something inside me tells me it's coming. Then I use my left hand—my best punch. I cut them up with it, and then I get to work with both hands.'

He would eventually retire and be a black preacher for his

people. 'They need so much,' he said, almost wistfully. A troubled look came into his eyes.

'They try to pretend "Swing Low, Sweet Chariot" is a hymn, but what it really meant for the black people was that they had visions of an army up there in the sky which will destroy the whites.'

His voice grew angry.

'Why do whites think they are superior beings? They have no right. There's thousands of UFOs waiting to come down on cities and blast the whites away.'

I looked at him and wondered was he putting this on. There was a boyish glint of fun in his eyes which dilutes his most ferocious statements.

How had he felt about the way he had been treated because he refused to be drafted into the US Army?

'I'll tell you something,' Ali said. 'I just went and did my own thing. My agent, Dick Fulton, sent me on lecture tours all over the United States. I got in a Volkswagen and travelled thousands of miles on my own.'

Wasn't it dangerous by himself in the deep South?

'I could be shot tomorrow if it's the will of Allah,' said Ali. 'A true Muslim doesn't fear, neither does he grieve. I was happier than I've ever been in that little car all by my black self—laughing, singing and tap dancing wherever I went. Fulton sent me down there in the middle of all those riots, but nothing happened. I was one black the State didn't get, who didn't sell out. I was no Uncle Tom.'

Just before the plane landed I got an insight into the champ's sense of public relations. As he recited his verse, some little boys in the seats in front were gazing back goggle-eyed.

Ali held up his hand majestically. The bard's flow was not

to be interfered with. Finally, one little Jewish boy, greatly daring, shoved the microphone of a tape recorder under Ali's mouth. For a second I thought the champ would explode. He jumped up.

'I'm going to hit you so hard you'll never get up. I'm gonna knock you right out of the plane, you great idiot. I'm gonna do to you what I did to Joe Frazier.'

It was only when I saw a delighted grin on the kid's face that I realised what Ali had done. He was giving the kid the thrill of his life by telling him on tape that a heavyweight champion of the world would knock him out.

As we walked from the plane at Kennedy Airport, everyone recognised Ali. Some reached out to touch him.

'It's hard to be humble when you're as good as I am,' Ali said as we walked past the fence. 'I'm good-looking. I can sing, dance, talk. I can box better than anyone else.'

He looked at me sideways, the same boyish glint of mischief—putting on.

There was a chauffeur-driven Rolls Royce to meet him outside. Ali offered me a ride to town. He introduced me to his broken-nosed companion, who turned out to be Kid Gavilan, former welter-weight champion of the world and master of the 'Bolo' punch. The Kid was down and out in Alabama recently when Ali discovered him and picked up the tab.

As we rolled into Fun City, the Kid started singing Spanish songs which he maintained he had written himself, while Ali's well-shaped head rolled from side to side in the front seat. The champ was out for the count.

The next time I saw Ali, he was looking bored as he got in the ring in a challenge fight against Jimmy Young at Landover, Maryland. He'd had too many fights that he knew

The Butterfly and the Baby

he couldn't lose and was only overweight from eating ice cream and cakes. But his wind was excellent, and his legs and arms in shape. Or they were before Jimmy Young, the 'no hope' challenger, got to work to take the great man the full fifteen rounds.

Ali won all right, by a unanimous verdict, but not clearly. Never mind, his entourage remains black and beautiful—some of the most gorgeous ladies in the United States, brown, black and saffron, every kink out of their hair, dressed out of Paris. Drama generates like an atomic reactor from the champ's room. In the afternoon, Governor Jerry Brown of California, en route to a pugilistic *putsch* in the primaries, called in just to have his photo taken with Ali.

Ali took so long to get up steam in the fight that in the end he could have lost. He just couldn't get through Young's guard. He missed completely with some right crosses, and had to resort to rabbit punches with the inside of the glove, a lazy man's tactic. Young can duck well, fade out of distance. His weakness is that he has a poor left lead, and stands square. He had never fought more than ten rounds before this, and Ali obviously felt he'd chin him around that time.

In the ninth round, Ali got up off his heels on to the balls of his feet, always a sign that he's sniffing around for the kill. Dancing to the left, he flicked out ten left jabs in succession. But they didn't get him far. Points—but no damage. By round eleven he was down on his heels again. Plodding after Young and concerned about winning.

Then, in round twelve, Young was up on his toes and starting to move around as if cheered by his discovery that he could last the distance. He was weaving well, and Ali, throwing in some vicious crosses, missed with all of them.

In the thirteenth round, it was Young who put in the right

crosses, and twice he landed smack on Ali's chin and shook him. In the fourteenth, Young definitely set the pace with more right crosses that hit the target, and a left-right combination that had Ali confused. In the last round, Young seemed so pleased to have lasted the distance that he took no chances with Ali's terrific onslaught, and just stuck his head through the ropes, where he couldn't be got at, as things hotted up. Previously his maximum earnings for a fight were £3,500, but when he left the ring this time he had earned £42,000.

Afterwards, Ali admitted that Young had dazed him. A significant phrase slipped into Ali's monologue: 'I could see Youth facing me.' That is the spectre haunting every champion who has been there a long time—of a fighter with fire in his belly who wants to win more than the champ himself does.

In a preliminary bout, Ken Norton had ripped Ron Stander to pieces with a fusillade of uppercuts that would have taken the head off a hippopotamus. Ali must know he's on to a toughie here. (Norton broke Ali's jaw in 1973.)

During the boring parts of the fight I was grateful for Elaine. I discovered her of all places purring at my feet. She was one of the beautifully dressed black girls who had been around at the start, but there had been a mix-up and she hadn't been given a seat, so she sneaked into the press area and coiled up like a comfortable cat under my table peering up at the fight.

I uncoiled her after my foot bumped against her and offered her the press seat next to me. She announced to surprised pressmen that she was covering the fight for the *Virgin Press*.

Then she showed me some photographs of herself and Ali.

The Butterfly and the Baby

She was 5ft 11in. The colour of coffee ice-cream and luscious. Some journalists behind us shouted at her to sit down when things got exciting—one of them for some reason was covering the fight for *The Economist*—and she turned and fixed them with a look of sweet contempt: 'If y'all don't stop shouting, I'm going to have to ask you an embarrassing question about your mothers.'

Sometimes an elevator can be a real help. I'd had a lot of trouble trying to fix a meeting with Ali. The heads around him had changed since we'd last met. There were two of these in the elevator last night at 2 a.m. Spirotechnical hair and shiny shoes. They said Ali was going to talk to the press at eleven next morning and after that he would see me in his room.

Next morning I am watching Ali doing an Oscar Wilde on the world press for two hours. He was witty, amusing and eloquent and gave an Actor's Studio performance of the character he has invented for himself.

True to his word, he was upstairs in his room five minutes afterwards. I was sitting beside him and observing that in his bare feet (he had taken off his shoes) he still gave an impression of Michaelangelo's David, perfectly formed except for an incongruous twisted toe-nail on his right foot.

Just as we started to talk, the door opened and two enormous jocks came in with a tiny little black lady between them. She wished to speak to Mr Ali. After three days waiting, was I going to be upstaged? It appeared that her daughter had had a car accident a year ago and was now paralysed, unable to move or speak. Could Mr Ali say a few words to her on the telephone. Yes, he would speak to her. Would someone dial the number. The woman put her hand into his to explain that, as her daughter could not speak, she would have to reply to Mr Ali by giving two taps for yes on the phone and one for no. The heavyweight champion of the world leaned back like a resting Atlas, and spoke for fifteen minutes about God and hope and love, to the stricken girl, while she replied by tapping her pen against the mouthpiece.

As he led the lady to the door, I noticed that she was so small that when he put his arm round her shoulders, she only reached the tip of his fingers. When he came in, the Butterfly was back once more in the dancing mood. But I knew that nothing I would learn about him could tell me more than what I'd just witnessed.

Randy Neumann is a handsome six-foot white American with prospects in Hollywood. He is also doing well as a writer. What is unusual about Randy is that he is a heavyweight boxer who has been ranked sixth in the States and who had a victory over Jimmy Young, who scared the pants of Ali by nearly beating him in Washington.

Randy is the 'Baby Hemingway' of the Lion's Head. This is the writers' bar of New York—Christopher Street, in the West Village—where Norman Mailer, Barbra Streisand, Pete Hamill, Dwight McDonald, Wilfred Sheed, Shirley MacLaine and David Amran hang out. When I got there in 1976, the news is that Randy is going into the ring again after a twelve-month lay-off in an elimination bout for the world TV championship series.

There was a party for Randy at the Lion's Head two days before the fight. Randy was looking chipper.

'I have just given my first novel to my publishers and they like it,' he told me.

Jimmy Young is due to fight Foreman next month in an

elimination bout for the heavyweight title and if he wins the fight Randy would be in the reckoning again.

I asked him how it felt to be a contender. Randy flashed one of those smiles which have made him the darling of women editors of the New York magazines. (*Viva* magazine once printed fourteen photographs of Randy in the shower.)

'I get $10,000 for this fight and if I win the series $50,000. That's going to help me do a lot of writing and acting.'

Then another of those smiles which drew a deep sigh from a blonde girl right behind me.

'Oh, Randy, these photographs in *Viva*! Why did you get yourself photographed in the next issue with a girl? I tore you up after that.'

Randy was smiling like a strobe light and the girl was clinging on to him when I moved off to get my ticket for the fight. The entire writing fraternity from the Lion's Head were going out the next day in a bus to New Jersey to cheer for Randy.

Everyone was excited as the bus headed off. It would be nice to have a writer-champ about the bar again. There was a lot of beer in the bus and people seemed to be smoking something that smelled sweet.

The atmosphere at the fight was like something out of a 1930s' movie. Guys were standing up in their seats shouting and there were large men chewing cigars. In the back seat was an enormous blind man with a seraphic smile on his face who cocked his ear to the roar of the crowd as he listened with the other one to an account of the fight from a pal next to him. An MC with the face of a well-made corpse announced the fight in funeral tones. There were boxing groupies in the front row who kissed and shrieked whenever their favourite boxer went on a rampage.

When Randy's fight against Sailor Arrington was announced a surprise was that Angelo Dundee, Muhammad Ali's trainer, was in the Sailor's corner. The Sailor was a tough-looking customer with a chin which seemed to be permanently stuck to his chest.

In the first round Randy came out with classic straight lefts knocking the Sailor's head back like an Aunt Sally. It was like Muhammad Ali against Jean-Pierre Coopman, the flat-footed Lion of Flanders.

Randy danced around on his toes as his opponent flailed at him. I don't know if boxers think of such things during fights but if Randy won this one he could be in line for $50,000. Then in the second round disaster struck. Suddenly Randy's left eye seemed to have been designed by Francis Bacon. He had taken a butt from his opponent which cut him right across the eyelid. At the end of the round the seconds monkeyed around with him, but it was clear from now on that he couldn't see from one eye. He wasn't able to judge his distance. The vital thing for a boxer is to get into distance. This means choosing the right moment to hit as an opponent moves around. If the punch is thrown from too far out it loses half its power. If the boxer waits till he gets too near, his opponent will get there first. Judging distance in the ring is as delicate as timing a golf swing.

In fact, I learned afterwards that it was worse, Randy had double vision. In the fifth round with a half-blind man in the ring, the referee stopped the fight.

I went into the dressing room to see Randy. He didn't look downhearted at all, though his right eye was a red blotch.

'I have really got a sense of relief. There's no way you can avoid this in a fight. Every time I go into a ring I can meet a

Bozo like Arrington who will cut me up. Now I can plug back into my acting and writing activities.'

On the way back on the bus they weren't talking too much. Someone said Randy had always been a cutter. Against Chuck Wepner, who went fifteen rounds with Ali for the world title and knocked him down once, Randy was ahead by five rounds when the fight stopped because of a cut eye.

Back in the bar there wasn't much talk about the fight either. A film director was on the phone explaining to the operator he wanted Istanbul not Englewood Cliffs. Someone else was saying Manson was innocent. They would have to save up their talk about this fight until it became a legend. It would be a long time before the Lion's Head bred another 'Baby Hemingway'.

ROYAL, ANCIENT AND EXASPERATING
Vincent Banville

My first set of golf clubs was bought from Harry Bradshaw. The Brad was professional at Portmarnock at the time, an avuncular figure, with an avaricious gleam in his eye. The clubs were second-hand but serviceable, I was shown how to hold them, then sent out for a round. I got lost, caused a dozen golf balls to disappear into the wild blue yonder, and came in foot-sore, exhausted and mad as hell.

It was the early summer of 1963 and I was due to do a second tour of teaching in Nigeria. Take up golf, I'd been advised on my first tour, it's a game for colonials, along with cricket, polo and serial fornicating. Asked, when I was home on holiday, if I were a lay missionary, I replied, 'No, more a lay mercenary'.

There was a country-wide strike on when I arrived at Port Harcourt. My golf clubs, of course, caused uproar.

'Why you bring in guns?' an outraged customs official asked me. 'Who you go shoot?'

'No one,' I protested. 'These are golf sticks. For play on a golf course. Eighteen holes, fluidity of swing, poetry in motion, head down and follow through on the green. You must be familiar with the game ...'

Despite such civility on my part, and an extraordinary show of patience, I was not allowed to decamp. My bag of golf clubs was impounded and I was informed that an army explosives expert was being called in to investigate the contents. Afraid that he would blow them up, I resorted to the good old system of 'dash'—called bribery in other parts of the world—and eventually was allowed to depart.

The Shell camp in Owerri had been evacuated by the oil executives, and the mission people had been given free run of its amenities. These included a club house, a swimming pool and a nine-hole golf course. The course had been cut out of commonage, so people still felt free to disport themselves on it. The result was a constant stream of casual traffic: women carrying their belongings on their heads, their male partners ambling lazily along behind them; members of the Fulani tribe herding their long-horned cattle; naked children doing what naked children do; and OPW workers scattered idly about like groupings of Rodin statues.

All of these, at one time or another, had to be circumnavigated by the intrepid golfers of the lay mission society. Instead of greens, we had browns, small areas cut out of the surrounding terrain and overlaid with sand impregnated with axle grease. Rock-hard underneath in the Dry Season, when a ball landed on one of them it would bounce exuberantly into the air and disappear into the surrounding bush, while in the Wet Season, the same stroke would find the ball stuck firmly in a slush as stickily adhesive as porridge.

The job of caddie was eagerly fought over by a raggle-taggle of small, bare-footed boys. The one who adopted me was called Bonaventure. He had a shaven head tattooed by whorls of ringworm, enormous eyes, an infectious grin and an instinct as larcenous as Bill Sykes's.

The caddies knew that if their master won, there would be an extra tip in it for them. This resulted in them resorting to more and more ingenious ways of cheating, the most common being that when they came to their players' ball they would grip it under the toes of their bare feet and walk along unconcerned for an extra fifty or a hundred yards.

My fellow, Bonaventure, had an extraordinarily prehensile set of such appendages, so the length of my drives became celebrated in song and story all over Eastern Nigeria.

I had many an eventful round on that golf course in Owerri, the more eventful as it fell into disrepair. After the Shell people left, the maintenance of the course fell to the local council and, as can be guessed, it did not come high on their list of priorities. I played quite a lot with a small, orotund priest who used drive me mad by coming out with advice like, 'Use the number five iron, my man', when I knocked down a shot. He would then use that same club to rip the ball unerringly onto the green and slot the putt to win the money yet again.

He did have a great fund of stories and once assured me that on a memorable occasion his drive at the long fifth had gone straight up the fundament of a Fulani cow, which had then taken off at a gallop, squeezed out the ball beside the green, from which position good Fr Joe had chipped in for an albatross two. He then ruined the story by commenting, 'If you believe that, you'll believe anything.'

My days in Nigeria drew to a close, but not my fatal attraction to golf. In my youth I had been quite an accomplished hurler, but was too cowardly to progress very far in such an abrasive sport. Tennis became a passing fancy, then squash. But the lure of the golf course always drew me back.

The game is constantly being denigrated by non-players—'A good walk spoiled', etc.—but I think they miss the point. A four-ball is always good fun, when you combine with a partner, but it is in singles play that the true test of character is definitively analysed. It is when you are standing alone on a plateau, silly tea-cosy hat on head, a gale blowing up the legs of your wet suit, the rain like little arrows stinging your eyeballs, and you've got to make a one over par for two points to win the monthly medal, that the refrain of, 'Are you a man or a mouse?' really does your head in.

I was once in a position of being thirty-seven points up with two holes to play on a nine-hole course in Edenderry. I had shots on the last two holes, so a pair of fives would see me with forty-one points and the Spring Lamb within my grasp. However, when we had been called through on the short seventh in our first nine, a character known as The Gloom Merchant—for obvious reasons—had been searching for his ball in jungle country. Lo and behold, when we came round again, some couple of hours later, he was once more poking about in roughly the same place. When one of my playing partners said, 'Good God, Bob, are you still there?' I started laughing so much that I made a mess of the following holes and was pipped by one point for the juicy hind quarters of that bloody Spring Lamb.

The beginnings of golf are hidden in the mists of time and legend, but historical fact has it that it was a game of national importance in Scotland before Christopher Columbus was born—I wonder what his short game was like? So popular was it during the 15th century that in March of 1457 the parliament of James II, who was at war with England, issued a decree declaring the game illegal because it was interfering with the archery practice of the soldiers.

Both of Scotland's Stuart kings, its queen, and all four British kings of that House were golfers. It's said that Charles I, in fact, was playing on the links of Leith when word was brought to him of the Irish Rebellion of 1641, and back in 1567 Mary Queen of Scots was criticised for playing a round within a few days of the murder of her husband, Lord Darnley.

The word 'golf' is derived from the Germanic word *kolbe* meaning simply 'club'. Beyond that, the game is entirely Scottish in nature—just like the Scots to foist such an ulcer-inducing game on the rest of the world—although the English dispute this and insist that they were the originators. In early times the ball was a leather bag stuffed with feathers and it was hit with a bent stick.

At first it was played by the Scottish middle- and lower-classes on linksland: sandy deposits left by centuries of receding oceanic tides. Constructed by nature, rather than man-made, these rain-swept and wind-whipped courses were fertilised by bird-droppings, while bunkers were formed by sheep and other animals burrowing their way into the turf for warmth. Can it be that playing under such adverse geographical conditions was the reason the Scots took so eagerly to drink?

It was with the formation of The Society of St Andrews Golfers—which, after receiving a royal charter in 1834, became the Royal and Ancient Golf Club of St Andrews–that the spread of golf courses proliferated. As the game became popular, refinements were made to balls, clubs and equipment, a trend that continues to the present day, and one tht makes serious inroads into the financial resources of easily influenced practitioners.

It is in this present century that golf has really taken off, the exploits of the professionals in particular having truly caught the public's fancy. And television has served to spread its popularity. Now a billion-pound industry, it is responsible for reams of reading matter on how to play it, fashion on how to dress for it, and equipment on how to get that extra length, extra draw, extra putt.

The professionals and the best amateurs, of course, play a different game from the run of the mill adherents. My own handicap has fluctuated erratically from 18 to 17 and back again in thirty mainly frustrating years of tramping the fairways. I have experimented with a myriad of different swings, different body positions, different stances. I've broken clubs, thrown them into lakes, cursed them, stamped on them, given them away. And I can't remember the number of times I've taken a solemn vow never even to think about golf, never mind play it.

But I always return to it, buoyed up by a tip from that twelve handicapper with the prosthetic knee whom I play regularly and seem never able to beat, or by reading a new book by yet another expert who assures me that golf is basically a simple game and that 90 per cent of it is in the head. My problem is that my body never seems able to do what said head tells it.

I regard myself as a reasonably intelligent human being, yet over and over, where golf is concerned, I make the same stupid mistakes. How many thousands of times have I turned my body to the left, sending my drive out of bounds? How often have I lifted my head, duffing a simple chip and ending up in that bunker that certainly wasn't in play a moment ago? Will I ever learn to stroke the putt, rather than jab at it like a demented beginner with an alcoholic twitch?

And the rules of golf! Ye Gods, even Niccolò Machiavelli himself couldn't have come up with a more convoluted, abstruse and baffling set of dos and don'ts. I was once disqualified from a competition for taking a practice putt on the third green of a nine-hole golf course, yet if it were an eighteen-hole track I could have done it with impunity. You can't touch the sand in the bunker with your club, you can't improve your lie, you mustn't break or in any way damage living growth.

Yet there is no game at which it is easier to cheat. The hole in the trouser pocket for dropping balls in the rough after the one you originally hit cannot be found. The half-dozen fresh air shots that you conveniently forget to add to your score card. Tipping the ball forward when you stoop to mark it on the green. The inadvertent sneeze just as your opponent is at the top of his back swing. Remember the marvelous golf sequence in Ian Fleming's *Goldfinger*, when the eponymous villain tries to con Bond and of course is beaten at his own game.

Strangely enough, although there are mountains of factual books written about golf, it hasn't featured a lot in the fictional sphere. Other than PG Wodehouse's *The Heart of a Goof* and *The Clicking of Cuthbert* I can't immediately bring to mind any novels or short stories about the game. Similarly in the realm of film, I can only recall the two *Caddyshack* efforts and the recent Kevin Costner movie *Tin Cup*.

In the rollcall of great players, my favourites have always been Lee Trevino among the Americans, Ian Woosnam of the British brigade, and wristy Christy O'Connor Senior of the home-grown variety. Trevino, of the wide stance and flat swing, joked his way around courses, probably drove his partners crazy, and still contrived to win a hatful of majors.

Whenever I venture into the realms of gold and imagine myself as having conquered the infernal game, it's always Woosnam that I see myself as: small, compact, but with a simple swing that sent the ball miles. Perhaps his temperament wasn't all that it should have been, but that was a human failing that made me like him all the more.

Christy O'Connor was the most accessible to me of the world's great golfers, playing as he did, a large part of the time on home soil. I saw him carve out many great rounds, wonderful shots and exquisite recoveries. Just one of his many exploits that stays in my mind was at the third, I think it was, at Woodbrook during the Irish Open in the early Seventies. He hit his second shot onto the railway line and out of bounds. Nothing daunted, he dropped a ball, struck it to within a foot of the hole and sank the put for a one-over par five. But it was the nonchalance with which he did it that took my fancy. If only one could show the same fortitude of spirit in similar circumstances, not to mention execute the same shot.

The greatest modern swashbuckler of the golf courses of the world has got to be Seve Ballesteros, now unfortunately in decline, but the nonpareil when at his peak. He strode the fairways like a colossus, even though the majority of his great shots were struck from impossible positions off the fairways. Hogan, Faldo and their ilk were like automatons, grinding out immaculate rounds relentlessly and boringly, but it was players like Seve who lit the imagination and instilled rapture.

Caddies, a motley bunch in the early days and still a hardliving, hard-drinking crew, if the truth be told, have their own little niche where story and fable are concerned. Legend has it that when St Andrews caddies die they climb to heaven on a ladder from the first tee of the Old Course, marking the steps as they go with chalk for all the lies they've told. There were two famous characters called Lang Willie and Donald Blue and, when Lang Willie died, he met Blue coming down again. 'Why you comin' down?' he asked him. 'I need more chalk,' replied Blue.

Television, as I've already mentioned, has made golf popular all over the world, and in so doing has thrown up two of the best commentators on any sport that I've ever heard. The first was the venerable Henry Longhurst, whose hushed tones and gilded phrases made many a tournament memorable, while his disciple in modern times, the equally august Peter Alliss cannot be bettered where the succinct one-liner or the tellingly descriptive vignette are concerned. For example, when the unfortunate Tommy Nakajima, within sight of winning the British Open, took nine shots to get out of the formidable bunker on the 17th at St Andrews, Alliss came out with the unforgettable cognomen for said bunker, 'The sands of Nakajima'.

Which leads me nicely to the golf joke. Like all sports, golf is encrusted round by a myriad of bizarre happenings, funny incidents and outlandish tales. Most of these are locker-room stories, golf being still controversially a male-dominated game—but we won't go into that here!—and are too rude to print. One I heard recently, however, and that I liked, is the yarn about the grandfather, father and son who were about to set out for a round. As they stood on the first tee, they were joined by a curvaceous blonde, who asked if she might accompany them.

They readily agreed and, after a few holes, it turned out that the young lady was a most accomplished practitioner. As she stood on the eighteenth tee she was at level par, but, after three shots on this par four finishing hole, she was still some twelve feet from the cup. She immediately announced that she would sleep with whichever one of her partners could give her the correct line to the hole.

The son stalked the green and gave it as his opinion that the ball would come in from the left lip. Then the father had a lengthy look and advised her to stroke it in from the right. Without any perusal whatever, the grandfather picked the ball up, handed it to the blonde and told her it was a 'gimme'!

For the greater part of my adult life I've had a love-hate relationship with the Royal and Ancient game. But like most relationships, it is the chase, rather than the completion, that makes the blood sing. I'll probably never be any good at golf, but there's always hope, with a scenario something like the following:

A glorious summer's day, a sky of azure blue, an immaculate golf course, the smell of new mown grass, the trilling of the Willow Warbler. I stand on the first tee and slide one down the right-hand side of the fairway. Then a four iron of 180 yards to within twenty feet of the pin, and two putts for a safe par. I continue in that vein, par, par, then the odd birdy. God's in his heaven, all's right with the world and I'm having that once-in-a-lifetime day when everything goes right for me on the golf course.

It may never happen, but the possibility is there, and, if it does come about, for one bright shining moment I'll have walked with giants.

Fore!

IS FOOTBALL BETTER THAN SEX?

Joseph O'Connor

It is sometimes said, and said quite insistently, that football is better than sex. At first glance, this seems a strange and highly debatable statement. The two activities are so completely and utterly different. One involves sensuality, passion, emotion, commitment, selflessness, the speechless admiration of sheer heart-stopping beauty, rushes of breathtaking, ecstatic excitement, followed by shattering, toe-curling, orgasmic pleasure.

And the other is sex.

Certain women who are not football fans—I am reliably informed that there are one or two such creatures left in the world—sometimes fail to understand the subtleties of this connection. They simply do not relate emotionally to the blissful anticipation of the game, the sacred ritual of preparation, the joyful build-up to the great event, the veritable foreplay that is the brisk booing and tribal barracking of the opposing team and its supporters, the plateau phase of the contest itself, as it thrusts first this way, then that, the mounting excitement ... HE DRIBBLES!! HE SHOOTS!! HE SCORES!! ... and the shared ... er ... climax of victory, with the attendant spontaneous overflowing of pride and raw emotion, not to mention beer.

At this point, let me say to women readers: It is not that he *prefers* his football to you (although, if I were you I would hesitate for a moment and think very carefully before forming the question in such a way that he might have to choose between one or the other). It is just that his football team is a bit better at playing football. You may well be the love of his life, the most open-hearted, beautiful, intelligent, fabulous, caring, sexually enticing woman he has ever been blessed to meet in his entire miserable excuse for an existence. Look, you may be *the mother of his children*. But are you going to make the World Cup finals? No. Be honest. Not even if you train very hard and adopt the flat back four formation. And if you did, you couldn't even beat one of the minor teams, such as Iran, South Africa or Scotland. (Well, OK then, maybe Scotland.)

It is true, of course, that not all football fans are men. In recent times, more and more women have come to the realisation that their mothers were completely wrong about this, that football is a wonderful thing. Far from being happy about this development, many men are actually threatened by it, and quite rightly. In the old days, you knew what a girl thought about football. It was crap. It was boring. It was unpleasant. It was about as quintessentially male as you could get without the aid of illegal hormones. But now things are different. As more and more women switch on to the game of two halves, you now face the very real possibility that your girlfriend may know a good deal more about the sweeper system than you do. Imagine! Women discussing blistering runs down the line, pinpoint accurate crosses into the box, devastating power headers! It is all quite horrifying.

Everyone knows that in the past football provided the perfect focus for that most important and sacred of courtship rituals: male droning. This is an absolutely crucial factor in any lasting heterosexual relationship. Male droning occurs when the male drones on and on and on *ad nauseam* about nothing important and the female switches onto emotional auto-pilot, nodding understandingly and throwing in the occasional frown of interest while secretly thinking about something else. It is particularly pronounced in very young men and very old men, but a completely drone-free male is so rare as to be considered officially extinct. Good subjects for male droning include:

- teenage children, poor examination results and employment prospects of
- lads in the office, considerable drinking capacity of
- all politicians, fundamental uselessness of
- God, existence or none-existence of
- modern popular musicians, inability to write a tune (not like in our day)
- "this", what he may or may not have done to deserve
- your mother, eerily unpleasant odor of
- the dog, elimination of, if it tries to fuck the sofa just one more time

But of all subjects for male droning, football is probably the very best.

That's how Mother Nature intended it. From time immemorial that's how it has been. I expect that if we really could decipher those early French cave paintings the archaeologists discovered recently, they would say: CAVEMAN ONE: 'Now, dear, you see if the player is *in front* of the ball when it is played, then he is *offside*. Whereas if he...' CAVEWOMAN TWO: 'I wonder when he will get up off his arse and go discover fire.'

But to return to my central point: the tired old accusation is, of course, that men prefer football to sex because they are not particularly good at expressing their emotions. They don't

Is Football Better Than Sex?

show their sensitive side. They don't talk about their feelings. They don't cry. (Believe me, when you support Aston Villa, you cry till you get to *like* it.) And let us be fair, I don't know where this argument comes from. Yes, all over the country this coming season, the same scene will be re-enacted again and again. Two couples will get together to spend a sociable evening in each other's company. The women will talk about relatively unimportant things, such as the destruction of the rain forests, the depletion of the ozone layer and the almost amusing remoteness of the possibility of human life continuing on the planet for very much longer. And then, at a certain point in the proceedings, one of the men will surreptitiously glance at his watch. Then at the other man. Then towards the door. Their eyebrows will twitch. Small, almost imperceptible nods will be exchanged. They cannot help it. We are dealing with the call of the wild here. Like tiny, confused woodland animals obeying the command to hibernate, both men will slowly, inexorably drift into the other room to watch an international football match, played by two countries they have never been to in their lives and could not find on a map even if their very souls depended on so doing. But to argue that they will not be sharing their emotions would be quite wildly inaccurate. 'That was never offside,' they will say. Or, even, 'Give me another beer.'

The sad truth of the matter is that, for some men, in the match between sex and football, there is ultimately no contest. Let us look at the simple facts of the thing, for Heaven's sake. A game of football lasts for a whole ninety minutes! And afterwards, you can invite your friends around, get in a pizza and watch it all again and again on video, pausing the screen to look at the most exciting bits in slow motion. What could be better! I mean, yes, I suppose you

Joseph O'Connor

could do that with sex also. I know *I* do. But you run the risk that it might affect your relationship just a tad, for example when the wife arrives home early from her mother's, with the parish priest in tow. Phew. Nice to see you, Father. Put down that collection box and pull up a chair, why don't you, there's a really good bit coming up.

Sex, the Italians say, is the poor man's opera. But like a lot of other things the Italians say, this is not true at all. Football is the poor man's opera. There, on the side of the classic stage of the perfect pitch, in the immortal gaze of the floodlights, is all the passion, emotion and excitement—not to mention sheer physical violence and bloody awful acting—of a Puccini masterpiece. Only it's better. What musical maestro could have invented a character as insolently noble as Eric Cantona, as dashingly heroic as Michael Owen, as brilliantly flawed as David Beckham, as cruelly, villainously precise as Jurgen Klinsman, as fat as Paul Gascoigne?

You want music? We got it. For awe-inspiring passion, sheer beauty, poetic majesty, how could Verdi's 'Chorus of the Hebrew Slaves' ever possibly compare to the famously rousing hymn with which supporters of South East London's Millwall FC so sportingly and welcomingly serenade the fans of their opponents: 'You're Goin' Home in a Fark-in' Ambulance.' Did Wagner ever pen a line that could beat 'Ooh. Aah. Paul McGrath, Say Ooh-Aah, Paul McGrath'. And where in the collected recordings of Callas and Domingo can you find anything that contains a sentiment expressed with the terse Yeatsian precision of 'The Referee's a Wanker. The Referee's a Wanker. Ee-Eye-Adio, The Referee's a Wanker'.

But quite apart from its artistic appeal, there are other reasons why men like football so much. There is a lot of talk

Is Football Better Than Sex?

these days about how football's real attraction is that it makes supporters—particularly men, threatened, emasculated and robbed of gender identity by the tremendous advances of feminism, such as equal pay, equal rights and the push-up bra—feel included in some sort of huge extended family of fandom. Once upon a time, men left behind their womenfolk and lumbered off to the battlefield or into the primeval forest together to bang drums, chant bloodthirsty slogans and paint their faces the colour of vomit. Now they go to the football stadium, where they can also get hot-dogs, hamburgers and an assortment of expensive souvenir items.

There is an important spiritual dimension also. Professors and thinkers and contemporary commentators of great intelligence (also Jimmy Hill) have posited that the central dramatic narrative of football has about it something of the power of great fiction, the ability it confers to step outside the self for a temporary and defined moment, the conveying of the sacred right to belong to something larger than one person, a communal and unified entity which finally becomes more than the sum of its parts. This is a point of view with which most male football fans would enthusiastically concur, by loudly saying the word 'huh?'

People will sometimes tell you that such a desire is a little unhealthy and xenophobic, or even potentially fascist, that we must all struggle bravely to build a world without borders or tribes, a world of maturity and tolerance, where our children, not to mention our children's children, will live in mutual understanding and harmony for ever more. And that is, of course, fine. Once we beat the Germans.

We must always remember that football is the most truly democratic game of all time. Indeed, it is the only genuinely international game there is. Almost totally unencumbered by considerations of class or geography or social standing, it is played on street corners, in car parks, on vacant lots, and in massive stadia, in every corner of the globe. It is as universal as Coca Cola and the Roman Catholic Church, but not quite as bad for your health. Go to any Third World country and you will certainly not find the local children playing croquet or polo or golf. (Not that golf qualifies as an actual sport so much as a stomach-churning form of masochistic torture, but you take my point.) You don't need a swimming pool, a nine iron, a graphite racket, a horse, a noseful of cocaine or any of the other items so many sports seem to demand these days. A ball and a couple of shirts to act as goalposts, and you are, as they say in the West of Ireland, suckin' diesel.

For all the corruption of owners, the venality of managers and the Machiavellian scandals that have haunted and beset the beautiful game in recent years, all the greed of agents, the manipulation of players, the tragedies of Hillsborough and Hysel, the insane hatreds of the lunatic fringe of hooligans, football is one of the last great public embodiments of the human spirit of innocence. Bill Shankley was once asked whether he saw football as a matter of life and death. "Oh, no," he replied, "it's much more important than that." But I like to think that he was joking. If not, I like to think that he was wrong. Because what is ultimately important about football is that it is ultimately not important at all. You can dress it up as much as you like but in the long run, it is twenty-two rational, sentient human beings (and sometimes Vinny Jones) chasing an inflated bladder around a field and kissing the face off each other when they kick it between two bits of wood. The fact that people can get so over-excited about something so fundamentally stupid is really one of the most marvellous things you could imagine. Sex is quite stupid

Is Football Better Than Sex?

too, when you look at it closely, as I often do. But then, you do not win the Jule Rimet trophy for sex. Unless you are very good at it indeed. I have never even won a book-token for it myself.

I know many women feel that men are infatuated with their football teams. But that is quite laughable. I mean OK, perhaps they were *once* infatuated with them, just as they were infatuated with other seductive aspects of teendom, such as heavy metal music, flared trousers and born-again Christianity. All these provided temptation to men when they were younger and more silly and impressionable. But over time, their youthful feelings about their football teams have grown into something more meaningful and lasting and mature. Yes. Love.

A man may love a woman—indeed, he does, as often as possible—but he can get *involved* with a football team in a more deeply spiritual way. A football team does not leave its tights and bra on the bathroom floor. A football team does not shave its legs using his special razor (although it would be quite welcome should the need ever arise). And perhaps most important of all, a football team does not keep going on and on *ad nauseam* about how great and handsome and wonderful George Clooney is, when everyone knows George Clooney has never played football in his life and is, consequently, only a man in the strictly biological sense.

So do men really prefer football to sex? Well, no, of course not, although it does sometimes appear that way; certainly, it may seem a slightly sad state of affairs when the answer to the question, "Darling, what's your favourite position?" turns out to be, "Centre half". But then, it is vital to remember that many men do actually believe that their personal support of a football team is in some way vital to its sporting success, that

Our Lord in Heaven has given them the power to influence the outcome of football games by shouting loudly and dying their hair the colour of their team shirt and vigorously casting aspersions on the proclivities of the referee's mother. This is all quite nice for men, as sometimes they do not seem to have the power to influence the outcome of sex very much.

Yes, it may seem strange, mysterious, inexplicable to a woman that her man can truly care in the very deepest core of his being about eleven individuals he does not personally know, and who almost certainly do not give a sparrow's fart about him, when she, despite her best and continuing efforts, can't even get him to get his hair cut and stop biting his toenails. But hey, try and understand him. Get involved. Make a little effort. As the fine and wise singer Billy Bragg once so poignantly asked, 'How can you lie back and think of England, when you don't even know who's on the team?'

I know it can be annoying. A man can sometimes appear to his partner as though his main interest in life is getting a bit drunk and reciting the names of all the players who participated in the FA Cup Final of 1931. But be gentle and patient with him. If you dig down really deeply, and bring him a ham sandwich, you will find that actually, what he is *really* interested in, on a more profound and existential level, is getting a bit drunk and reciting the names of *all* the players who participated in the FA Cup Final *ever*. And then wondering why he never did. And then crying for his Mammy. And then going to sleep.

This is, of course, the marvellous thing about men, or at least, about male sports fans. As a general rule, they do not have large numbers of terribly deep feelings about anything much, and when they do, they don't want to think about them or analyse them at great length. This is probably the category

Is Football Better Than Sex?

that you women readers are in. Listen, he idolizes you. He worships you. He has put Georgie Best on his fantasy football team, but he has put you on a pedestal. He loves you so much that most of the time he simply can't figure it out. Put at its most basic, you are the best thing that has every happened to him, and he adores you. But he *understands* football. And perhaps above all else, a man such as the one I have described here needs something to understand.

It's a close-run thing, but football, better than sex with someone you love? Ha! No way in the world.

Unless, of course, it is played by Manchester United. Then we are into a different league.

666 ON THE DEVIL'S GOLF COURSE
Sara Berkeley

'What does the desert mean? It means what it is. It is there, it will be there when we are gone.'
Edward Abbey

'Minerals crytallize out of solution as they reach their individual solubilities.'
Pamphlet about the geology of Death Valley

First we walked on sand. Lots of animal tracks up into the dunes. After that, texture after texture as the salts changed; like snow, like the Arctic without cold. Then medallions, giant brittle plates that lifted at the edges sometimes six or eight inches off the ground and threatened to break my ankles if they cracked. Then, closer to the centre, big structures, knobs and jagged crystalline outcroppings. The main saltpan was sludgy, muddy under the crusted surface, and so white in the relentless sun that my eyes hurt even behind sunglasses. It was like walking on another planet. I had to keep reminding myself: this is *Earth*. Out the other side of the saltpan, the salt rings began again, stretching across The Devil's Golf Course towards the Black Mountains that divide the Amargossa Valley from Death Valley itself. We walked nearly twenty miles, but I scarcely felt it, and I'm not super fit by any stretch of the imagination. The surroundings simply soaked up all my attention. The silence took me out of my body, out of the world, and gave me utter calm.

The next day, after we'd broken our camp in Hanaupah Canyon and were leaving the valley through Furnace Creek, I glanced at the odometer. We'd set it to zero at the start of our trip. It said 666.

A couple of months after this trip, I received an e-mail inviting me to contribute to *Playing the Field*. Four thousand words on sport. I jumped at the chance. That night, I woke with a jolt. *Sport?* What, a treatise on my brief career as a hockey wing? All I can remember of hockey is intense anxiety in case the ball came my way, because I could never figure out from the frenzied little stick-bashing episode at the start which direction to play in. This sporting handicap seems to run in my family, because a brother once came home from a football match and told Mum that yes, it was great, but he was a bit confused about which goal was home. And my nephew, seven now and flapping about in his giant soccer outfit, might enjoy the game more if it didn't interfere so badly with his private dancing sessions over on the sideline. My middle brother really carries the baton for the whole family with his athletic pursuits. So what the hell could I write about sports?

Then I eyed my shelf of diaries and thought about the many roadtrips they chronicled. What had I been doing every long weekend, every Spring Break, every chance I got since coming to America but discovering the great outdoors, the Wild West, the five superb, astonishing deserts of the western United States? Wilderness camping's a sport, isn't? Eh? If it wasn't, it is now.

When I say wilderness camping, I really mean off-road car

camping. Let me gloss for the uninitiated, or anyone who thinks I'm one of those heroically fit types who hoist fifty-five-pound packs on their backs and disappear on foot into the bush for weeks. Car camping means you bring all your gear in the car, and that your gear can include a two-foot thick air mattress if you so desire. Off-road means you turn off those long smooth strips of asphalt and take to dirt tracks where the gravel is ridged like a washboard, your major bones are generally shuddered out of alignment, and the desert begins at last to unfold around you in all its vast emptiness. Off-road car camping means you can probably see your car when you unroll your sleeping-bag that night. If you do it right, in Nevada or Utah particularly, it can also mean that your car is the only car you see for two, three, sometimes four days. This, to me, is true sport—'amusing oneself in outdoor physical recreation' in its purest form.

The truth is, I hate competition. I don't like coming last, I don't like coming first, and it's peculiarly dull to come anywhere in between. Competitive sport tends, in my experience, to bring out some of the worst traits in the animal that is us. Greed, envy, egotism, and the desire to punch another man viciously about the head and neck. (Do they have women's boxing yet? I don't have a TV.)

I know there's decent competition. Before steroids, the Olympics brought tears to my eyes, it was so... Olympian. And every Monday night football match brings delight to scads of Americans. I want my kids to have a healthy competitive spirit, to learn how to win and lose with grace. It's just that I hate that tension, that lining-up-waiting-for-the-starter-gun feeling. What if I'm worse than all the rest? What if I'm better? What if I'm *the same*?!

Before I become too existentially nauseous about such a

simple concept, let me return to the slickrock plateaux of Canyonlands National Park, Utah. There, in the early winter of 1995, my husband and I drove so far down a trail that was so heavily strewn with rocks of such giant size that I was sure we would be discovered there in the spring, a pair of grinning skeletons, bolt upright in our Nissan King Cab, each clutching a topo map of Horsethief Point. No, wait: *he'd* be clutching the map. *I'd* be clutching a note scrawled in bitter red biro: 'He said the road got *better*.'

It's not that I blame my husband for all our reckless scrapes. It's horribly easy to get into very bad situations when you leave the main thoroughfares of America. Look at that chap in *Bonfire of the Vanities*, for instance. (It's probably time to instruct my mother to stop reading this essay at once. I didn't tell you quite all my camping stories, Mum. It was for your own good.)

I particularly like remembering the dizzy, roughly-hewn trail that winds down into Labyrinth Canyon, at the heart of Canyonlands. I was learning the names of the rock strata: Navajo sandstone, Kenyata foundation, Wingate sandstone, Chilne formation. I recited them as we crawled down the tortuous trial because it kept me from being scared to death. In the valley below, quiet as the valley of death (before the six hundred), we found a single signpost. Moab, 21 miles to the east. Hanksville, 34 miles west. Pinned to the signpost was a sun-bleached flier: 'Lost dog. Answers to Max'. The mystery of how you could mislay a dog in that empty, echoing wasteland has never been satisfactorily cleared up for me. Max must have really despised his owners.

I sat on a rock in the silence and thought of John Wesley Powell and his boatmen, sliding down the Colorado River in the summer of 1869. Powell had a habit of scrambling up the canyon walls whenever he could. From the top, he would catch a glimpse of the surface of the country through which his boats traveled in crevices sometimes a mile deep. 'By now', wrote Wallace Stegner, chronicler of the journey in *Beyond the Hundredth Meridian*, 'they had left behind them all familiarity; the country was such as none of them had ever seen. On the broken plains stretching away from rimrock there was no vegetation, only worn rock and sand and the bizarre forms of desert erosion; in the distance, the Roan Cliffs were pale azure, the flat and tabular outlines of mesas and buttes were evenly bedded, coloured like the rainbow. It looked like unknown country.... They named it Labyrinth Canyon'.

Climbing back up to the other side of the canyon, looking down over the bare edge (*'white rock, organ rock, cedar mesa...'*), I told my husband in a hushed voice to stop the truck. We got out and peered over the precipice. Forty feet below, under a huge pile of rubble, two vehicles clung rustily to the cliff side. We joked nervously about skeletons, got back in our rented Jeep, and crawled onwards round the gravelly hairpin bends. My only regret is that I forgot to take a photo to send home. 'Having a great trip—met with slight accident—not too many broken bones—Sara.'

Then there's the Mojave, and the art of camping in the sand desert, where every cup of coffee comes with silicon whether you take it that way or not. We entered it from Interstate 15 at Baker, where the Bun Boy Motel boasts the world's tallest thermometer. It commemorates the hottest temperature ever recorded in the United States: 134°(F) in Death Valley in 1913. About twenty miles north of Baker, on a cold November day in 1996, we turned onto Cima Road and entered Shadow Valley. A hideous accident just outside town had paralyzed the highway for miles and we had to crawl past the wreckage just before our turning. The sky was red, and the valley was full of Joshua trees, dwarf trees with grotesquely twisted limbs that over time I have come to see as beautiful. After the carnage on the highway, it was eerily peaceful. We drove deep into the desert and stopped to camp when the lights of Baker were no longer visible and the dunes were already turning many, many shades of pink and orange. Over in the west, the sky was violently streaked, and in the valley we were bathed in light. It was palpable, I could feel it washing over us. I remember feeling incredible joy.

But the desert is a place of extremes, and just a few hours later my mood had plummeted dramatically. As the light faded, we realised it was going to be too cold to sleep out in our 20° sleeping bags. So, reluctantly, we broke camp and packed up the truck. Coming in, the road had been downhill in places. Now, according to the laws of Intensely Frustrating Physical Truth, it was uphill. We got stuck. It took half an hour to dig the truck out (an unpleasant activity, preferably not to be attempted without a team of slaves) and then an increasingly scary drive down a maze of different roads trying to find one with less than four inches of sand. It had been a windy day. We'd drive along gravel, see sand ahead in the headlights, get out with the flashlight, walk on, see how deep the sand was, how long it went on for... Then another ten-point turn on the narrow desert track, and another road we couldn't be sure we hadn't been along already. It took us four hours to get out. But hey! That's Sport!

Back to the Bun Boy and The Mad Greek for burgers. One real advantage of wilderness camping is that it gives you a warm appreciation for even the lowliest of motels. You don't have to shake your shoes for scorpions when you get out of bed in a motel. (I *told* you to stop reading, Mum!) You don't have to embark on a multi-layered programme to warm up when you rise to see the dawn. You just step in the shower. However, remain in no doubt that the benefits of sleeping under the stars far outweigh the odd life-threatening insect. There are the coyotes with their weird staccato howling back and forth across the valleys. There's the passage of the sun across the wide-open sky, and the Coming Out Ball that is a clear night's star show. Moonshadows. On endless pristine sand. Constellations you begin to recognize; their journeys— intricate criss-crossings of the night sky... 'This most excellent canopy, the air... This brave o'erhanging firmament, this majestical roof fretted with golden fire...' Well, I'd have said it that way if Hamlet hadn't beaten me to it.

Waxing lyrical is hard to avoid when you sleep under the stars in the Great Basin desert. You want everyone else to have the experience too, and yet, paradoxically, you want nobody else to have the experience because being out there alone *is* the experience. After a day without any outside human contact, you begin jealously to guard the solitude. A column of dust from a car five miles away begins to seem like an outrageous intrusion. I've sat looking out over a vast, empty landscape and wondered was I still the same person who loves riding the London Underground and thrives on the excitement of international airports. All those *people*, when there's all this *space*. If, like Edward Abbey said, the desert will always be there, I think it's possible to have the best of both worlds. Keeping up with wilderness legislation in Washington, however, is a soul-destroying exercise. As with any pleasure, there are those intent on compromising it. But Senator Orin Hatch (Republican) and Congressman Jim

Hansen (Republican) shall remain nameless. Let's keep the politics out of sport.

Every game has its rules, and wilderness camping is no exception. Like some of the hardier sports (she explained modestly), breaking the rules can mean serious injury or death. I know, because luck has kept me alive more than once. The primary rules in the desert, at least during the summer months, are twofold. One: drink more water than you want to. Two: put on more clothes as the sun goes down than you think you'll ever need. Dehydration hits you long before you actually feel thirsty. I felt the beginnings of it driving out of Death Valley one May evening, 110° at 6 pm, and I'm glad I had the wit to keep drinking water long after my thirst was quenched and my headache subsided. History books tell stories of people emerging from the valley naked with their clothes held over their head in the delirious conviction that they were wading through water. So the name of the game is Survival, and if you ain't playin' Survival, you're in the wrong game.

I could tell the story here about how I nearly got hyperthermia on Castle Crag Mountain, but I *know* you're still reading, Mum. So maybe a discussion of the desert wildflowers? Yes, it's stretching the sport theme a little, but I can't resist. The desert wildflower is such a heroic example of life in the face of adversity. Let's say that poking about in the Great Basin desert in wildflower season is my version of watching the paraplegic Olympics.

If the name of the game is Survival, Skeletonweed gets the gold. When the rain is over and there's no more moisture to be found, Skeletonweed turns into a brittle brown bush that breaks off and blows away. It's a small cousin of the more famous tumbleweed, which, interestingly, is not indigenous to the Western states at all, but was introduced in the last century from the Russian steppes. Some fleeing revolutionary must have got a seed stuck to his dagger.

Wildflower season in the desert is brief and not as dramatically colourful as the flower books lead you to believe. There are splashes of colour: red Desert Paintbrush, tall yellow feathery Golden Prince's Plumes, the yellow knob heads of Basin Rayless Daisies. But the sand, rock and shale are all-pervading. It would take a flower population a thousand times denser to make any visible impression on the landscape. The joy is in close observation. The slower you walk, the more the colours show themselves. The cacti flowers are my favourites. Prickly pear, yellow and pink, waxlike petals; scarlet Claret Cup cactus. And receiving my personal Medal of Honour for survival against the odds is the Joshua tree. Fertilized only by the yucca moth, whose sole source of food is pollen from Joshua flowers, tree and moth lock each other in perfect symbiosis. Sex in nature: so simple, so safe.

Long distance runners and short sharp-shooters like racquetball players are always rabbiting on about endorphin highs, so I'm going to wheel out my wilderness camping equivalent. My endorphin rush is that feeling that wells up in me as I put the miles between me and the highway, and the desert closes quietly around me. It's the warm gritty wind on my skin, the comfortable dustiness of old shorts and a singlet, and what I would like to think of as the desert state of mind. Time slows. There are no plans, you live inside the moment. An ant crossing your foot as you sit drinking coffee is an event. And places like Lunar Lake, Nevada, exist just for you to discover, spend an astonishing couple of days in, and leave as you found them.

On Lunar Lake there are no wildflowers. No trees, no shrubs, not even any grass. I found a single dead bush hanging on in the middle of the dried lake bed when I ran out there, the ground the consistency of soft dry mud, crumbling like curry powder, perfectly kind to my bare feet. I could run with my eyes closed. I ran backwards for a while, trying to override the internal conditioning to check over my shoulder for obstacles. There were no obstacles. Back at camp, lying out on my air mattress with a cold beer, I watched the *playa* turn purple first, before sunset, then dark pink. After the sun set, it turned dark silver. We took photos, but it could not be captured. That night there was a full moon. Lunar Lake shimmered like a bridal veil. It was bittersweet breaking camp the next morning to return to civilization. We saw a coyote, clearly identifiable through the glasses, loping and stopping to forage and loping on. Then, as we drove out past the Easy Chair volcanic crater, a badger scrambled awkwardly up the bank at the side of the road, unmistakable when he looked back at us, with the white stripe down his forehead. He waddled off into the sagebrush where I saw his white stripe flash for a second, then he was gone.

Coming home from the desert along Interstate 80 through the ugly Sacramento valley, there is always a reluctant shift back to 'real' life. Soon, it will matter again where the house key is, whether your clothes are clean, which friends you haven't called in a while. Life crowds back in where there was space, and life is too fast. The best thing about the wilderness is how it reminds you that nothing, nothing, nothing on earth matters enough to be miserable or anxious over. Lying in a tent with the stars out around me and the immense silence behind the small sounds of the wind in the creosote bushes, or the squeak of dry twigs, or the scuttle of something, I know there is always the wilderness, where life is leveled. The difficulty is remembering during the in-between parts what it's like to be out there; what the canyon walls look like with the sun setting on them; the whorls of dead juniper; the feel of walking on slickrock; the silence, filled with all the noises that belong there. How the tables turn: everything that looks worthless at home becomes valuable. A water-bottle, a small camping stove, a flashlight. And things that seem important back in our lives—a wallet full of green notes and cards—are worthless, get stuffed down the bottom of the bag, of no use, no value because they can't dig or light or wash or warm.

'Wilderness is not a luxury', wrote Edward Abbey, laureate of the desert, in *Desert Solitaire*, 'but a necessity of the human spirit, and as vital to our lives as water and good bread. A civilization which destroys what little is left of the wild, the spare, the original is cutting itself off from its origins and betraying the principle of civilization itself.'

I remember an April afternoon a couple of years ago, scrambling out over slickrock and sandstone boulders to Panorama Point, some forty miles from Highway 24 in central Utah. I stood up there in the whipping wind, looking at the 360° view. Below me was the Maze, a labyrinth of switchback canyons falling away in layers. To the north, the La Sal mountains; to the south, the Henrys; to the east, the Abajos. Mountain range after mountain range, canyon upon canyon. It felt like the end of the world, and at the same time, like the origin, an original landscape without trace of human presence. I stayed there a long time just looking, and the rest of the world receded, unimportant. I knew that I would revisit that place in memory, and that the memory would fade and grow indistinct. But I was there, in that moment, and it was worth everything.

CONTRIBUTORS

BANVILLE, VINCENT was born in Wexford in 1940. He is the author of the *Hennessy* series for young adults and the novels *An End to Flight* (1973), *Death by Design* (1993) and *Death the Pale Rider* (1995).

BERKELEY, SARA was born in Dublin in 1967. Since she left Ireland in 1989, she has lived in London and the San Francisco Bay area, where she now works as a technical writer. She has published three collections of poetry: *Penn* (1986), *Home-movie Nights* (1989) and *Facts about Water* (1994). In 1992, she published a collection of short stories, *The Swimmer in the Deep Blue Dream*. Her first novel, *Shadowing Hannah*, was published in 1999.

CRONIN, ANTHONY was born in Enniscorthy in 1928. Best-known as a poet, his many publications include novels, essays and biographies of Flann O'Brien and Samuel Beckett. His account of 1960s literary Dublin, *Dead as Doornails*, has recently been reissued. In 1983, as adviser to then-Taoiseach Charles Haughey, he created Aosdána. For a number of years he wrote for *The Irish Field*.

GLAVIN, ANTHONY was born in Boston in 1946 and first moved to Ireland in 1974. A former editor of 'New Irish Writing' in *The Irish Press*, he has published two collections of stories, *One for Sorrow* (1980) and *The Draughtsman and the Unicorn* (1999), and a novel, *Nighthawk Alley* (1997).

LUSBY, JIM was born in Waterford in 1950. A schoolboy soccer player with the local Hibernians club, he was selected for the Waterford Youth team in successive seasons, 1967-8 and 1968-9. His work includes short stories, plays and documentaries. His series of novel, featuring the Waterford-based detective, Cal McCadden, opened with *Making the Cut* (1995; televised by RTE 1997) and continued with *Flashback* (1996) and *Kneeling at the Altar* (1998). He is currently working on the fourth in the series, *Crazy Man Michael*. As James Kennedy, he has also written the thrillers *Armed and Dangerous* (1996), *Silent City* (1998) and *Dark Witness* (due for publication in 2000).

MCCANN, COLUM is the author of a collection of stories, *Fishing the Sloe-Black River* (1994) and the novels *Songdogs* (1995) and *This Side of Brightness* (1998). His latest book is *Everything in This Country Must* (2000).

O'BRIEN, GEORGE was born in Enniscorthy in 1945 and reared in Lismore, Co Waterford. Among his publications are three volumes of autobiography—*The Village of Longing* (1987), *Dancehall Days* (1988) and *Out of Our Minds* (1994). He is Professor of English at Georgetown University, Washington, D.C.

O'CALLAGHAN, CONOR was born in Newry in 1968. His first collection of poems, *The History of Rain* (1993), won the Patrick Kavanagh Award and was shortlisted for the Forward Best First Collection Prize. A second collection, *Seatown*, appeared in 1999. He has also published many reviews in magazines and newspapers both in Ireland and the UK. His radio documentary on Irish cricket, *The Season*, produced by Dick Warner, was first broadcast in 1996 and has since been repeated many times. He is married to the poet Vona Groarke. They have two children, and live in Dundalk.

O'CONNOR, JOSEPH was born in Dublin in 1963. He has written three novels, *Cowboys and Indians* (1992), *Desperadoes* (1994) and *The Salesman* (1998); a book of short stories, *True Believers* (1991); two collections of humorous journalism, *The Secret World of the Irish Male* (1994) and *The Irish Male at Home and Abroad* (1996), and various other works, including a number of stageplays and filmscripts. His work has been translated into twelve languages. He once broke his ankle in two places while playing football.

O'CONNOR, ULICK was born in Dublin in 1929. His many books include biographies of Oliver St John Gogarty and Brendan Behan, and *Biographers and the Art of Biography* (1991). His *The Celtic Dawn* (1984) deals with the Literary Revival. He is also a poet and playwright. Some of his writings on sports have been collected in *Sport is My Lifeline* (1984). He was undefeated British Universities boxing champion.

O'MALLEY, MARY was born in Connemara in 1954. She has published three volumes of poetry, *A Consideration of Silk* (1990), *Where the Rock Floats* (1993) and *The Knife in the Wave* (1997). Her numerous awards include three Arts Council Bursaries. She was Mayo County Council Writer-in-Residence for 1995-6. Amharclann de hÍde commissioned her play *An Striapach Allúrach* (*The Foreign Whore*), and a fourth volume of poetry, *Travel Arrangements*, is forthcoming. Mary O'Malley is a member of Aosdána.

WALL, EAMONN was born and raised in Enniscorthy. He has published two collections of poetry, *Dyckman-200th Street* (1994) and *Iron Mountain Road* (1997). A book of essays, *From the Sin-é to the Black Hills*, has just been published by the University of Wisconsin Press. A third collection of poetry, *The Crosses*, is forthcoming. He is Professor of English at Creighton University, Omaha, Nebraska.